# A Companionable Silence

Hannah Winstone

Published by Trellis Publishing, 2021.

A COMPANIONABLE SILENCE

**First edition. July 4, 2021.**



ISBN: 979-8224865390

Written by Hannah Winstone.

# A COMPANIONABLE SILENCE

HANNAH WINSTONE

# A COMPANIONABLE SILENCE

Hazel eyes flickered across the paper held tightly in slender hands. Even though the woman who read it knew each word so intimately, more so than if she had written it herself, she found it impossible not to read it over and over again.

Janet Hough was a mail order bride, travelling half way across the continent to meet her husband-to-be for the first time. This letter, their last correspondence, was all she had of him - that along with a tiny photograph of him also encased in the same envelope. He was handsome, even if there wasn't much to see from such a small photograph; dark hair, clean shaven save for a dusting of stubble across his chin. A wide jaw and full lips that dimpled in the corners.

He was her ticket to a new life, a life where she was free to make her own choices, a life away from her unloving family and the shame that she had carried with her for the last three years.

The train whistled, loud and shrieking in her ears and Janet was wrenched from her thoughts. Startled her gaze shot to the window - only to see a dark, barren station outside. The train slowed to a stop, whining loudly as it juttered on the tracks. And then she was there.

The letter was carefully folded and inserted back into the envelope, then tucked away in the pocket of her heavy coat. She wasted no time in heaving her suitcases from underneath her seat and stumbling over her own feet to exit the train.

The station smelled of coal and heavy, dirty fumes - Janet's face twisted into a grimace as the overpowering smell hit her. Around her the station stretched on, huge but empty. She had arrived at an odd time, almost ten o'clock, and it showed in the cold settling into her joints and the eerie silence engulfing her.

She let her gaze wander, though there was not much to see; at least until her gaze landed on a tall, broad shouldered man. He appeared from behind a pillar, a large hand leaving the warmth of his pocket to wave. Janet knew him *instantly*, warmth overtaking her chest as she recognised the sweep of his dark hair, the set of thick brows.

As he approached Janet felt a grin overtake her soft features, hazel eyes widening in delight. He was *there*, finally within reach - but her legs refused to move, her whole body stuck in place. If she moved even just an inch she *swore* her legs might give out.

The man - Ezekiel, her *fiance* - smiled as he rushed to her, but he grinded to a halt a respectful distance away. She noticed how he fidgeted with the hem of his coat, how he seemed so unsure of stepping closer.

So Janet closed the distance for him. The suitcases lay abandoned and forgotten as she moved to him, her own grin growing until it felt as if her face might crack. "Ezekiel King?"

"Janet Hough?"

She nodded so furiously that loose strands of golden-red hair fell in her eyes, but she made no attempt to sweep them away. "Yes, it's me! Oh, I've been waiting for this for so long, and the journey here was so *stressful...*" She was babbling, that much was so clear and her face flushed as she realised how terrible a first impression she was making. "I'm sorry," the words fell from her lips, "I'm not meaning to complain. I just - this is all so incredible it hardly feels real."

Ezekiel's smile was polite, restrained - but his eyes sparkled. "I must confess, it's all a little unbelievable for me too. I spent most of today in a trance." He offered out a hand to take her bags, lifting them with ease despite the fact Janet had stuffed in as many of her belongings as possible. Then he offered an outstretched arm.

Janet linked her own tiny arm through his without hesitation. "You must think me odd, marrying a man I do not even know just to get away from my family." She flushed darker then, and was silently thankful that the dark station kept her face shrouded.

"Then I must be odd too," Ezekiel shot back with a nervous laugh, "for *I* am marrying a woman I do not know because I saw her advert in the paper."

A laugh escaped Janet's lips and she smothered it with her free hand. "I think perhaps we are *both* strange, but given the circumstances I wouldn't say that as a negative."

They walked in companionable silence, arms linked and paces slow. As they stepped out of the station and into the cool night air, Janet turned her face to the sky, enjoying the breeze against her skin. "Are we going to your home?"

"It's *ours* now; but yes. It isn't far; I thought we could walk?"

"I would enjoy that."

So they did, strolling down the streets together and enjoying the evening. Although Janet was hundreds of miles away from home warmth had settled in her gut, contentedness washing over her as she fell into step beside Ezekiel. She supposed it made sense; her home had never been a warm or loving place, and she had only made that worse for herself as the years went by.

This, however, was something new. A new place, a new *beginning*, something unknown and exhilarating. This was a chance to make things right for herself. Perhaps, once she settled in and got to know her husband, she would be safe enough to tell him the *real* reason she had left her family and life behind.

That was all a long way ahead for them both. For now she was content just to walk beside him, to feel his strong arm against hers and imagine what her new life had in store. The rest was going to take time, and perhaps that was all right. Janet was a patient woman, and she had already come this far, had she not?

———————————-

If there was one thing Janet loved about her new home, it was the chance to be treated as an equal. As the days passed she settled into a routine; she woke early, as did Ezekiel, and the two ate breakfast together before beginning their work on the ranch. Ezekiel was a patient teacher, appreciative of the assistance and eager to help her learn his way of life. It was so different from her quiet, meandering village life. She was kept busy; and was all the better for it.

Which was why not a single complaint passed by her lips as she struggled with the box of tools in her hands. Slender arms, not yet used to tough ranch life, strained and protested and her joints ached. With a gasp she let the box collapsed back to the ground with a *thud*. Disappointment settled in her gut but she pushed it back. It was impossible for her to adjust to this life in only a few days - so she had to be *patient*, and try her best.

"Jane; are you all right?" Ezekiel appeared behind her, strong but gentle arms spinning her until she bumped against his chest. Although her cheeks burned, he did not notice. "If it's too heavy we can find something else for you to do. You *know* I appreciate the help, but I hardly think it's worth hurting yourself over."

"I know," Jane replied with a sigh. She forced a smile but it was stilted, false. She risked peeking up at him through thick lashes, but there was not even a *hint* of annoyance on his softly smiling face. It brought a small, genuine smile of her own to ghost across her lips. "I just... I want to be *helpful*. I came here for the opportunities, the chance to prove myself-"

"You have nothing to prove," Ezekiel interjected with a laugh. A hand brushed across her hair as Ezekiel leaned close, and he drifted his lips gently across hers. "You have done *more* than enough for the ranch - for me - since you arrived on Friday, and you have every right to let yourself rest and settle in *properly*."

If only it was so easy. This new start was for her, yes, a chance to get away from the embarrassment and secrecy of her old life. But it was also for someone else, someone Ezekiel could *not* know about just yet. So she kept her lips tightly sealed and simply nodded.

"Is something wrong?"

Of course he sensed something wrong. Ezekiel was too kind and too observant not to notice her worries. A small sigh escaped her throat as she wormed out of his embrace - but she cast him what she hoped was a reassuring smile. "Not at all." Her lie was not even convincing to herself. Chewing on her lower lip Janet turned from him. "I am just tired. Perhaps I might take a small break before I tackle the next task."

"Then I will break with you."

"No, I-" Janet caught herself, then simply nodded. "Of course."

They sat together on the porch, overlooking the fields. The horses roamed freely rather than being confined to stables, and Janet watched idly as one wandered to the fence.

They sat in silence, too. Janet had been taught that silence was *negative;* awkward and tense and, more often than not, filled with shame. Silence meant no one wanted to talk to you, acknowledge you, that something was *wrong.* As she watched Ezekiel, however, she realised this simply wasn't true. He smiled gently, ankles crossed casually as he sat beside her. He looked *content.*

So Jane kept quiet, locking those thoughts away.

After a beat Ezekiel turned to her, his smile growing. "Janet, there is something I would like to tell you."

Her chest skipped, pulse skipping in her throat as she turned to him with wide eyes. "Oh?" She forced her voice to remain calm, but it was impossible to miss the way it wavered. "What is it?"

"Well..." He laughed, an awkward little sound that would have brought a smile to her lips had she not felt so uneasy. "I admit I don't know exactly how to say it but - well, I am happy you're here. I confess when I asked you to travel here - and what a long way it was! - I did not think much beforehand. I had hoped for a wife, of course, and company - but now I feel as if I took advantage. I wanted you here for myself, and I did not think of you at all. It was selfish, not to consider your feelings at all. I apologise."

Oh. Relief flooded her and she sank into the little wooden seat with a sigh. That's all this was about? "I came here of my own accord, did I not? It benefits the both of us."

"Of course." Although his acceptance was comforting, the pinch in his brows was not. "I hope you don't think ill of me. I feel as if I took advantage, without even meaning to. And then to keep my true feelings a secret..."

If he thought *that* was a secret, then he did not know the meaning of the word. How would he feel - what would he *think of her* - if he knew what she was hiding? The thought caused a chill down her spine and coldness to settle deep in her gut. Janet shivered.

"Please, Ezekiel, do not think anything of it," she replied, clipped. Suddenly the breeze felt too chill against her skin, the seat beneath her too hard and uncomfortable. Standing, she turned from him. "We should carry on with our work, otherwise we will never be finished in time."

"Janet, is something wrong? Please, do not be angry-"

"I'm not, I promise; but I would appreciate no more discussion of this."

———————————

Janet's pen glided across the paper as she wrote, back hunched over the old desk tucked away in Ezekiel's study. Every so often her hazel eyes flickered up to the door and she half expected to see him standing there, watching. He was outside working, so of course he wasn't going to appear in the doorway.

Even so, Janet couldn't shake the uneasy feeling in her stomach. A chance for peace was so rare, and a chance to actually sit down and write without interruption was even rarer. The risk of Ezekiel seeing her was too great; and if he saw he would start to ask questions. She had told him she had no family back home, but that wasn't true.

Rosie. Her daughter's name was Rosie, and Janet had travelled across America to provide for her. If only it had been possible to take Rosie with her; but Ezekiel couldn't know she had an illegitimate child; not if she wanted to stay here.

Not if she wanted him to trust her.

Pursing her lips Janet folded the letter, slipping it into the envelope along with a handful of money. It wasn't much, not nearly enough, but it would do for now. Once Janet found a proper job in town, and once she was sure Ezekiel wouldn't be suspicious, then-

"Janet."

Her head snapped up and a gasp escaped her lips as she shoved the letter out of view. "Yes, Ezekiel?"

"I am going into town - I was wondering if you would like to come with me. Are you writing a letter?"

Janet shifted, eyes darting down guiltily to glare at the envelope in her hands. "I am."

Questions. Now he was going to ask *who* she was writing to and Janet didn't know if she had an excuse. She should have known this never would have worked-

But Ezekiel only nodded, smiling softly as he leaned across the desk to place a soft kiss to her cheek. "If you've finished, we can leave now? Or if you want to finish writing we can wait."

Relief settled in Janet's stomach and she nodded, hair bouncing. He had no idea, none at all. Thank goodness! With a sigh she stood, shaky on slender legs, and said, "we can leave now, I don't mind. I shall post the letter while we're in town."

If Ezekiel was at all suspicious, he showed no signs. He linked an arm through his as they moved through the hall and into the sunny afternoon outside.

The way into town was silent, thick and awkward but only for *her.* It seemed as if just her company was enough for Ezekiel and he held no expectations for her. It was a concept that made her gut twist; but also that brought the warmth of relief spreading through her. She was conflicted.

Ezekiel left her to post the letter in private, wandering to the cluster of market stalls in the town square. Janet took her time posting the letter; in fact she hung back long after she was finished at the post office just to avoid going back to Ezekiel.

The problem wasn't that she didn't like him; he was a *wonderful* man, so kind to do all of this for her even if he believed in his 'selfish' reasoning. The problem was that Janet didn't know how long she could keep up the pretense. She planned to have Rosie back with her eventually; then what? What would she *tell him?*

With a sigh, Janet pushed back those thoughts and forced them to the back of her mind. Then she made her slow journey to the marketplace.

She found Ezekiel talking to a woman and her husband, their lips spread wide in cheerful smiles as they crouched over a baby carriage. All Janet saw of the child inside was a burst of bright ginger hair and round, flushed cheeks.

"Ah, Janet!" Ezekiel's eyes met hers and he beckoned her over with a wide grin. "These are my friends, Annie and Jeremiah Thomas - and *this* is their son, Sam."

"Good afternoon; it's lovely to finally meet you." Mrs. Thomas - *Annie* - smiled broadly, though her hands did not move from the baby carriage as she gently rocked it back and forth.

"G-good afternoon," Janet stuttered back - only to cringe at how *silly* she sounded. Her panic earlier had completely shot her nerves, and for no reason at all! She was *fine,* and Ezekiel none the wiser.

"They had little Sam just in January," Ezekiel continued, beaming down at the tiny baby all swaddled in white blankets. "People seem to think I am too old to have children now, but I haven't lost hope."

"You're *never* too old to start a family," Jeremiah chimed in with a laugh, "Sam is our first, and most of my brothers had several children by my age."

"Perhaps we *will* have children - but not now, of course." He flushed, deep and scarlet, and Janet couldn't help but notice how sweet he looked, so flustered like that. He was an easy man to like - and *yes,* Janet could see herself falling in love with him - but *children?*

"Perhaps," she answered cryptically - but her mind went to little Rosie. Just three years old and she had already been abandoned by her mother. Would Jeremiah love Rosie like his own child, or was he more likely to throw Janet from his home as soon as she told him the truth?

"Mrs. King?"

"Janet?"

Thrown from her thoughts, Janet simply blinked. Their words registered, but whatever they had said before was *lost* to her. "I apologise, I believe I was lost in thought."

Ezekiel smiled, as he always did, but it was tinged with worry Janet was not used to seeing. "I said we must get going; we have a lot to buy and limited time."

"Oh," Janet replied numbly, "of course."

They said their goodbyes and parted ways with the Thomas couple, but Janet couldn't ignore the dull, aching worry that had made itself at home in her chest.

For the rest of the day she was on edge, and even as she slipped under the covers and let her head fall against the pillow that night, she couldn't fight past it.

———————————

The morning after, Janet worked herself extra hard. When walking into town and inquiring about jobs earned no luck she got to work on the ranch, working her poor muscles harder than ever previously. When she stopped for lunch and Ezekiel asked her if something was wrong, she simply denied it and retreated to the stables.

At least in there, with only the horses tucked away for the evening, there was no one to judge her.

Until Ezekiel found her twenty minutes later and stood in the doorway with the setting sun casting shadows across his face and highlighting the gold in his bright blond hair. Even with his features etched in worry, he was dashing.

"Ezekiel," Janet acknowledged - but she did not look up from the saddle that sat heavily in her lap. A hand reached out for the polish as she dutifully removed the grime.

He hovered, unsure of what to do or say. After a moment he simply sighed and settled beside her on the little bench. To the left a horse whinnied, but he refused to take his eyes away from Janet.

Which, suffice to say, made her squirm and fidget as the heat rose to her cheeks. She itched to leave, or to ask *him* to leave, but she only pursed her lips and kept cleaning. Pretending to be fine became harder by the day; but she had practiced over the years. Just not through choice.

"Have I done something wrong, something to hurt you?"

The question left Janet speechless. Her mind flashed blank and she was left with now words, or the capability to speak them anyway. For a moment she only gaped.

"What I *mean,* is," Ezekiel began, and he ducked his head as if in embarrassment, "you have been acting strange, but now more so than before. If I have said something to offend-"

"You haven't said - or done - anything," Janet intercepted with a sigh. Discomfort bubbled in her chest but she swallowed it down. When she forced herself to meet his eyes it made her squirm, but she held his gaze nonetheless. "You have been nothing but wonderful, so please don't think otherwise."

"Then why are you avoiding me?"

Oh. So he had noticed. Janet winced, dark eyes flickering to the saddle in her hands. She couldn't deny it now; she needed an excuse an quick, something to put him at ease and stop him from inquiring further. What could-

"Was it what I said yesterday? I never intended to put you on the spot, especially in front of my friends."

That worked.

Janet shifted as she set the saddle aside, but still she didn't look at him. When she peeked out from the corner of her eyes she saw he wasn't looking at *her,* either. Was that better, or worse? Sighing she reached out to kiss his cheek, then ghosted it across his soft lips. Lying *hurt* - it hurt so much she felt as if someone was tearing out her heart - but it was for the best. She reminded herself of that as she said, "I suppose so. You mentioned children and I panicked. Don't you think it is far too early for that?"

"I suppose," Ezekiel concluded, though his eyebrows pinched, "I have wanted children for *so long,* and it has never been possible - a man my age has lost his appeal, and if not for you I would most likely never have married."

Janet winced. So *that* was the selfishness he had spoken of; he had seen her as a way to have children, to live the life he had assumed was beyond him. Even if it should have hurt, Janet felt only relief. "I understand - but we should wait until we know each other better. Live our lives together for a while before introducing a child."

Ezekiel nodded silently. Always so kind, so understanding - there was no doubt in her mind he would have done *anything* had she asked sweetly enough. Anything except, perhaps, help her raise a child born to another man.

Perhaps it had all been a mistake - coming here, expecting to leave all of her old worries behind and start a new life without consequence. As she looked into Ezekiel's eyes, however, and lost herself in his softly smiling face she *knew* that this was where she belonged. Not at home with her parents, who would have rather disowned her than let her keep her own child; or with her martyr sister who cared for Rosie despite her husband's protests of disgust. Janet belonged *here,* with her new husband and their beautiful ranch.

"Janet, are you lost in thought again?"

Blinking, she simply nodded.

"You do that often, don't you? Do you think you will ever let me know what's going on in your mind?"

Pursing her lips, Janet frowned. "There isn't any hiding it, is there?" She laughed - but it was dry, hoarse and without humour. "I suppose I should but... not yet. I'm sorry."

Silence. This time it *was* thick, tense with unsaid words and words Janet didn't even know *how* to say. It was the silence she had always hated, filled with shame and judgement. If only it was possible to just hide away, to ignore Ezekiel's judging stare...

When Janet forced herself to look up, there was no judgement in Ezekiel's warm eyes or kind smile. In one swift move he scooped her up to pepper kisses along her forehead, her cheeks, her jaw.

Laughter burst from Janet's lips as she shoved him away, tiny hands batting at his chest even if it did nothing. Eventually he set her down and she glared halfheartedly, smoothing down her skirts.

"You don't have to tell me now," Ezekiel concluded with a smile, "but soon, please? If it is something I can help with, I will."

Janet's forehead creased in a dainty frown, and for a moment she honestly considered telling him everything - but then her senses kicked in and she clamped her lips closed.

"Just consider it," Ezekiel suggested, his smile turning wistful. "I need to feed the pigs. I will see you at dinner?"

Janet nodded silently - and then she watched as Ezekiel stood, his back a silhouette against the vibrant pink of the setting sun.

Only when he was gone did she allow herself to breathe.

———————————

Once again Janet sat in Ezekiel's little office room, the oil lamp at her side burning low. It wasn't yet late, barely past dinner, but she had to resist her eyelids slipping closed. The stress of the last two weeks had finally gotten to her; it showed in the dark circles under her eyes and the slouch in her shoulders.

The fact that she had narrowly escaped telling Ezekiel the truth was only a small victory; she *knew* the time to tell him was coming soon. Too soon.

She dropped the pen to scrub at her heavy eyelids, leaning back in the wooden chair. It dug awkwardly into her back and it was far too unforgiving to get comfortable; it was perhaps the only thing stopping her from falling asleep right at the desk. With a small sigh she stretched, considering that perhaps it was time to call it a night; the letter would have to wait until morning-

"Tucked away in here, I see."

Her eyes snapped open and all traces of the sleepiness vanished. Slender arms fell to her side lifeless, but she risked a strained smile. "Don't mind me, I was just finishing up," came her hasty reply. She gathered up the letter with nervous hands - only to knock aside the pot of ink she had been using. It toppled, sending ink across the desk *and* the sleeve of her dress. Then it rolled and collapsed onto the floor with a dull *thud*.

Ezekiel was by her side in a second, scooping up the - thankfully intact - ink bottle at her feet. "Janet," he reprimanded; but there was softness in his voice. A forgiving kind of worry that Janet was so unused to hearing from *anyone* she knew. It gave her pause, heart warming. "There's something on your mind. Now, I know you don't like to talk about your problems - or *problem,* because I honestly believe this has all been about the one thing."

"Ezekiel-"

"Please let me finish. Whatever this is, I promise I won't be angry. If you are having second thoughts about this, or you are worried, I'll understand."

Second thoughts. He thought she was having second thoughts about their relationship? Oh, he couldn't have been *more wrong.* How could she not want to be with him when he was so sweet and kind and lovely? She had only known him a handful of weeks but she wanted so desperately for things to turn out all right.

When Janet didn't reply, Ezekiel rose to his feet. Although he dug around in the desk drawers to produce a cloth, he didn't look at Janet as he began gently soaking up the ink staining her dress. "You've put me in a difficult position," he commented softly, "how can I help if you do not tell me what is wrong? More to the point, how do I know this secret of yours isn't something terrible?"

It *was.* Not to her, because she loved Rosie with everything she had, but terrible for her reputation. For the people that knew her. For *Ezekiel* most of all. Janet took a deep breath, one that seemed to shake her entire body, and said, "it's something you need to know; but not now. I am sorry."

They petered off into silence. The office was silent save for their soft breaths and the rapid beating of Janet's heart. It rang in her ears, a sure sign of her guilt, and her head spun. There was nothing to do except watch as Ezekiel quietly cleaned up the desk. The cloth, ruined beyond repair, ended up in the little bin at their feet.

"Is it another man?"

The words rang in Janet's mind but they didn't register at first. She stared blankly, eyes squinting at his lovely face as she tried to decipher what he meant. When it clicked, she couldn't stop the gasp that broke from her throat. "Of course not! Why would you assume so; and how would I have found the time to seek out a man when I've been working on the ranch *with you?*"

"I don't know, but it's the only reason I can think of the secrecy. The letters, avoiding me for days, going so quiet for reasons I can't discern. What other reason is there?"

"It isn't a *man*," Janet snapped. She had *no right* to be so angry and she knew it; but at the same time it was impossible to stop the burning in her chest, the increasing desire to storm out without another word. Of all the conclusions, he came to that one?

Ezekiel pushed away from the desk, feet carrying him half way across the room before he spun back to face her. His face twisted in confusion, thick hands tugging at delicate, short hair. "Then *what,* Janet? I know I said I would give you time, but you cannot hide it forever. This affects me too, you understand."

"I do." That was the whole damn reason she hadn't said a thing! Couldn't he understand how much was at risk? If she told him he might toss her out, send her back home to face *more* shame than ever before. Then how would she provide for Rosie? A sigh slipped from her lips but it sounded more like a *growl*. Something damp and warm dripped onto her cheek - and that was when she realised she was *crying.* Janet never cried.

"How bad can it be, Janet? I have told you over and over that I will support you, that I won't be angry. What else can I do to convince you?"

Ezekiel waited for a reply. Janet couldn't force herself to provide one. Her throat closed up and her pulse quickened, roaring in her ears until everything else drowned out to nothing. By then the tears had clouded her vision, obscuring everything except for the fuzzy silhouette of Ezekiel standing in the center of the room.

"Fine. I cannot force you to tell me, and I won't try any more. Tell me when you're ready; or don't. Apparently, you don't think I deserve to know." He turned to leave, head bowed. Janet had never seen him so... *despondent,* so small despite his large frame.

"I have a child," Janet blurted without thinking. The words tumbled from her lips and once they began, she was helpless to stop it. "Her name is Rosie. My sister and brother-in-law care for her, because they are married and I was not, not when I had Rosie. My parents they... they tried to convince me to give up Rosie, and having my sister care for her was their *compromise.*" The word tasted bitter on her lips and she cringed.

Ezekiel hadn't moved. He stood so still he almost blended in with the furniture, body stiff and unyielding. With his back to her, his expression was a mystery.

"Ezekiel? I *knew* I shouldn't have said anything. I am *so sorry*-"

"You have a daughter?" He turned to face her, but even then his expression was unreadable. Eyebrows drawn, lips pursed and eyes downcast, it was the most conflicted she had ever seen him. Janet's gut twisted at the sight.

"I do," Janet replied, just because she didn't know what else to do. "She's three years old; four in August.

"And you weren't married at the time?"

The seat, cold and hard, made her back ache dully - but she didn't dare stand, didn't dare move closer to Ezekiel. "No, I wasn't. We had been courting for a few months. He wanted to... and I was too young to understand the consequences." Dropping her gaze, Janet's cheeks flushed and she wanted only to disappear forever. After all of this, she was surely going to disappear from his life, at least. He wouldn't want her now.

"Is that why you went so quiet when I introduced you to the Thomas' and their baby?"

A silent nod. It was all she was able to muster, hands clenched so tightly she was imprinting little half moons of her nails into her palms.

"It makes sense," Ezekiel admitted quietly, "and you left her, instead of bringing her with you?"

"I didn't know what else to *do!*" Janet snapped, "no one wants a woman with a child, especially not one conceived outwith marriage. She is better at my sister's, at least until I can get a proper job and find my place here."

"You already *have*," Ezekiel replied quietly. Once again he ran a hand through those beautiful locks. His glare slipped, sharp features relaxing until he only looked *exhausted*. Resigned.

Janet *did* approach him then, closing the distance between them with an outstretched hand and muttered apologies. He accepted her embrace without question, wrapping thick arms around her waist as she wrapped her own around his shoulders. When she pulled him close, pressing her face into the crook of his neck, she breathed in his scent. Musky hay and bitter late-night coffee, and salty tears.

Janet didn't know if those tears were Ezekiel's or her own. Perhaps both.

"I was just *so scared*," Janet murmured into his collar, "of what you might say - or *do;* but it isn't an excuse, I know that. I'm so sorry for all of this."

"As am I," Ezekiel replied softly.

It shot a stab of pain through Janet's chest and fresh tears bloomed. This time she didn't try to hold them back; she let them roll freely down her cheeks, staining both her dress and Ezekiel's shirt. Her shoulders shook, her sobs muffled as she pressed her face further into Ezekiel's shoulder.

He held her, gentle as if she were made of glass, and pressed the tiniest kiss to the top of her head. "I am not going to order you to leave, if that is your worry," he concluded with a sigh, "I have grown to love you over these weeks, you know."

Love. The word struck her chest and she sucked in a gasp, head snapping up. Love. It was far too early for that, too early to even *think* about it... but she had to be honest with herself. Did she not feel the same?

"You don't have to say it back to me," Ezekiel said with a smile, "just know it is true. I... thank you for telling me all of this, even though it was not really your choice. I pushed you too far."

"No," she replied too quickly - but as her cheeks darkened she continued, "you deserved to know since the beginning and I kept it from you. It was a silly and *cruel* thing to do." A pause in which Janet pried herself from Ezekiel's embrace, bright eyes flickering to meet his for the first time. "You're not angry?"

"I'm not *happy*," he replied with a forced smile, "but no, I am not angry. I understand why you might keep this from me, I am only upset you did not trust me before."

"Oh."

"Now, if that letter was for Rosie, why don't you write a new one? Tell her it's time she was reunited with her mother; and time to meet her step-father, too."

For a moment Janet could only stare - and then she grinned wide, flinging her arms around Ezekiel with a cry of relief. He lifted her effortlessly - and they both laughed, perfectly in sync, as he twirled her.

When Ezekiel set her down Janet pressed a kiss to his lips, revelling in the feeling of his soft skin against hers. She pulled away, still beaming so broadly and exclaimed, "thank you *so much!*"

Then she paused, her heart hammering in her chest and said, "Ezekiel? I know I never said it before but... I love you to. I can't wait for us to start our new life together. All three of us."

# REDEEMABLE

15

RICKI CROSS

## <u>Upstate</u>

He knew what it was before the courier got out of the van. Even the neighbors peering from their windows like buzzards for the carcass could detect the scent of complete annihilation. As the heavyset messenger lumbered up the snow-lined driveway and met him on the front steps, Patrick felt the sick sensation of defeat in his stomach and without a word, held out his hand to accept the manila envelope the man in the khaki uniform was handing him.

"Are you Reverend Patrick Dean?" the carrier asked. Swallowing the lump in his throat, Patrick nodded. "I need you to sign this, Mr. Dean. You've been served."

Without argument, Patrick took the pen and scribbled his name before retreating quickly into the house with the package before the tears flowed from his burning eyes. He leaned heavily against the door and exhaled slowly, trying to collect himself. Then, he moved to the staircase and sat down. With trembling hands, he tore open the envelope and read the dreaded contents. Cynthia had filed for a divorce. A divorce. The word reverberated through his skull like a bullet. Of course he had been expecting it but the reality was still almost too much for him to stomach.

Unsteadily, he rose to his feet. He tried to remember the last time he had eaten. He couldn't recall his last meal. That was probably a bad sign. He wiped his tired, streaked eyes and walked into the kitchen, determined to reclaim some of his former strength. His life may have been falling apart but he was still a strong man, a man of God and God would want him to live and fight another day. *God wouldn't want you divorcing your wife,* a snide voice in his ear whispered. Patrick shoved the thought out of his head and yanked open the fridge with too much force. A glass ketchup bottle fell to the floor and shattered. Jamba came running eagerly into the room, smelling food like the little scavenger she was.

"No! Get out of here before you cut your paw!" he commanded the bloodhound. She paused uncertainly and slowly backed away, giving him a hurt look. As he quickly cleaned up the mess, he realized that the ketchup he had just disposed of was just about the last staple of food left in his refrigerator. A scan of the pantry produced the same results. He needed to go shopping. He had been to the grocery store once since Cynthia had left almost three weeks prior. Shuffling into the hall, he ushered Jamba up the stairs and changed out of his robe into a pair of raggedy track pants and old sweatshirt. The dog looked up at him expectantly, her tail wagging. Patrick was overcome by guilt. When was the last time he had taken the pooch on a decent walk? He vowed he would do that when he got back from the store. He scratched her ears affectionately and grabbed his keys off the dresser, purposely avoiding the reflection in the mirror. He knew what it would show; a man riddled with shame and anguish.

Thankfully the snow had stopped falling during the night and only the white mounds piled on the side of the road were reminiscent of the two-day storm that had finally ended. As Patrick pulled into the small parking lot of the local grocer, he was relieved to find it almost deserted. It was a Tuesday morning after all. Hurriedly, he slipped inside and pulled a cart into the produce section. Without much regard for what he was selecting, he began throwing items in, hoping to be in and out before the inevitable occurred. Yet, as he rounded the corner into the condiment aisle, he almost collided with a young boy who was crouched near the floor, peering at the pickles with intense scrutiny. The child looked up at him, startled and then his serious expression melted into a huge smile.

"Pastor Pat!" he yelled. Patrick cringed, feeling the blood drain from his face. The boy ran over and threw his arms around the older man. Patrick gently hugged young Austin back and released him, looking around for his mother. As if on cue, she came storming up the lane and seized her son's hand, glaring viciously at Patrick.

"Pastor Pat where have you been? We keep looking for you at church but you don't go up on stage and talk anymore!"

"No, Austin, I don't do sermons at the church anymore," Patrick said quietly, averting his eyes from the woman's steely gaze.

"Oh! Why not? I like it when you tell the stories about the animals and the boat and the snake and the giant. The other Pastor is no fun. He just reads pages out of this big boring book." If Patrick hadn't been so depressed, he would have chuckled at the five-year old's interpretations.

"You should give Pastor Michael a chance, Austin. He is a very nice man," Patrick chided, chucking the child under his chin.

"More importantly, son, he is not a drunk, an adulterer or a sinner," Austin's mother chimed, pulling her son from Patrick's reach. Both Austin and Patrick blinked at her tone. Patrick's face turned crimson and as he excused himself, he heard Austin say, "Mom, what's a dalter?"

Somehow, Patrick managed to purchase the few objects he had tossed into the cart and make it home in a fog. When Jamba greeting him at the door, he completely forsook his promise to take her for a walk and after haphazardly throwing the groceries into the kitchen, he threw himself onto his bed and stared hopelessly up at the ceiling. *I am a pariah. This will haunt me for the rest of my life. I need to get out of here.* There was something cold and wet on his hand. Jamba had followed him into the room and was nuzzling his hand with a cold nose. He petted her head absently and as he sat up, his eyes fell onto a worn photograph on the dresser. Slowly, he rose to his feet and picked up the picture. While the frame had been there for as long as he could remember, he hadn't heeded its existence in years. Gently, he wiped the dust off the silver and smiled wistfully at his own happy expression in the image. He had been so young, holding a fishing pole and grinning without a care in the world. But it was the property in the background which held his attention. Patrick knew where he had to go.

**<u>Down South</u>**

It was just as dirty and dilapidated as he remembered. There were even more holes in the roof than the last time he had visited and at least one hurricane had eaten away at most of the siding. Thankfully, the cabin was miniscule enough that the contractor with whom he had spoken guaranteed a full repair in about a week but until then, Patrick and Jamba were going to be contending with the elements.

As man and dog slowly ascended the rickety steps, under the humble cypress trees, some feral animal mewled angrily and hissed from under the slats in the porch. Jamba yelped in fear but Patrick was overwhelmed with nostalgia of childhood. This cottage had been in his family for four generations. His great grandparents had built it and birthed all twelve of their children within its five rooms. His father had been born there, along with six of his aunts. After that era, the place had been used strictly as a getaway property for the cousins but as everyone aged and became successful, the majority of the family had left the deep south and ventured onto "better" things. Suddenly everyone had cabins in Aspen or summer homes in the Hamptons. It seemed that Patrick was apparently to only one who felt a kinship to the rundown house, despite its sorry state. Granted, he didn't spend the time he wanted in the bayou but he had always had a great affection for the property and its history.

The door was not locked and Patrick rolled his suitcase into the tiny front room which was both the kitchen and living room. Grandpa's antique rocker was still there and while there were spider webs in every corner, the potbelly stove was where he remembered, the tiny bar fridge was in the kitchen and even the wash basin was by the back door. *If this were the city, there would be nothing left. Someone would have stolen all the belongings and some squatters would be living in attic.* But this was not the city. This was the serene, trusting south where things were still sacred and people watched out for one another. He reached out and flicked a light switch but of course there was no electricity. He would have to tend to that tomorrow. Beside him, Jamba whined again. She was out of her element but the truth was, the reason Patrick had rescued her from the shelter was that she reminded him of one of his grandpa's hunting hounds. He had even named her Jamba for Jambalaya despite Cynthia's protests.

"What an awful name for a dog! It's bad enough that she's so ugly! Take her back and get something smaller and cuter, Pat!" Yet the dog had stuck and so had the name and it had truly been the only reminder Patrick had of his childhood in the womb of America. From under the rocker, a scared green snake slithered out and disappeared into a crack in the slat floor. Jamba howled and ran out of the still open screen door.

"Jamba!" Patrick dropped his suitcase and tore after her down the dirt road. He caught glimpse of her tail disappear around the corner and he rushed toward the bushes. Panting, he turned around the bend and stopped abruptly. Jamba was in the arms of a boy of maybe eight, shivering in fright. But behind the child and dog was a woman standing in the doorway of her cottage. Patrick could make out the tall outline of a black haired woman in a blue dress but he could not see her face. Even so, she took his breath away – or at least the little breath he had left after chasing his hound.

"Jamba! Come!" Patrick found his voice. Reluctantly, the dog slunk out of the boy's lap and retreated to his master. The woman stepped out of the home and Patrick's heart leapt into his throat as the beauty of her face enthralled him. She had big blue eyes filled with wisdom and compassion, a lovely cream complexion and a welcoming smile.

"I'm so sorry! She got frightened off by a snake. She's never seen one before," Patrick heard himself babble. The woman's smile widened.

"Well I understand that," she replied with a sweet Southern drawl which only enhanced her attractiveness. "She ain't hurting nobody ova here. Damien 'n I love dogs, don't we, honey?"

The young boy nodded eagerly, dark eyes wide but his lips did not move. The woman continued forward. She wiped her hands on the apron covering the skirt of her dress and offered a palm to Patrick. He accepted it and noticed how soft were her hands.

"Sarah Jane," she said. "An' this is ma son, Damien. Y'all ain't from around here. I kin tell."

Patrick shook his head.

"I'm Patrick. This is Jamba. We're from...out of town." Patrick was reluctant to give her too much information. The idea was to retreat from people, not make new friends to disappoint.

"We jus' moved here from Baton Rouge 'bout a year ago. Where y'all stayin'?" Patrick pointed down the road.

"In the Dean's place. It's my family's but no one much uses it anymore." Sarah Jane raised an eyebrow in surprise.

"Y'all can't stay there! All them 'coons and cats be livin' up in there now. It ain't safe nor sanitary!"

"I have contractors coming to fix it up. We won't be like this too long," Patrick assured her. He suddenly noticed Damien staring intently at him.

"How old are you, Damien?" Patrick asked. He had always liked children and they seemed to feel the same about him. The boy did not answer but he did not look away.

"Damien don't talk much," Sarah Jane said quietly. Patrick nodded understandingly. He smiled at the boy.

"Nothing wrong with that," he replied. "Still waters always run the deepest."

A look of surprise and appreciation flashed through Sarah Jane's lovely eyes.

"Why don't y'all get settled in and come back fer dinner. Y'all like gumbo? Ma pa always said I make the best gumbo this side of New Orleans."

"If it's all right with your husband. I wouldn't want to impose." Patrick almost choked on the word "husband." He had no idea what had come over him. He never had attractions like this to perfect strangers but for some reason he was drawn to this woman. *You need to walk away before you get yourself in even more trouble,* he warned himself. But his own warning went unheeded. Sarah Jane laughed throatily.

"If y'all kin find him, y'all kin ask him yourself," she chuckled. "We ain't seen Damien's pa since the boy was knee high to a grasshopper." Patrick wasn't sure if he was contrite or relieved. Probably a bit of both. "Y'all come at 6. Bring yer Jamba. I'll have a bowl fer her too."

Back at the shack, Patrick perched gently on his grandpa's rocker and began to sway back and forth. He was thinking about Sarah Jane and the sense that he had known her for a long while. He wondered if her black waves were as soft as they appeared. Guiltily, he tried to shift his thoughts but he couldn't seem to get her smile out of his head with the slight gap between her teeth and the endearing but almost inaudible lisp her mouth produced. Her eyes reminded him of someone...abruptly, Patrick sat up in the wooden chair, startling Jamba from her sleeping position at his feet. Shame stained his cheeks a scarlet he feared would never fade. He realized exactly why he found Sarah Jane so desirable; she was a physical combination of his wife and the woman with whom he had ruined the sanctity of his marriage.

### <u>Upstate</u>

### <u>*One Month Prior*</u>

*"I really have no interest in going, Cyndi," Patrick sighed as he finished tying his tie in the full length mirror. "I don't see why I need to be there."*

*"Oh Pat, you're marrying them next week. Just go, have a scotch, make a toast and come home. It's your duty to attend these events." Patrick sighed again and turned to face his wife, feeling a slight sense of jealousy. She was already in her pajamas, curled up in bed with her knitting. He knew she was right. Bachelor parties were a rite of passage and he was hosting the ceremony for the happy couple but he had never been a fan of the ritual. He was always secretly relieved when the grooms planned rowdy*

*gatherings and opted to leave him out of them. He would much rather be home playing ball with Jamba or reading a book.*

*Dutifully, he dropped a kiss on Cynthia's cheek and headed out of the bedroom.*

*"Please don't forget to let Jamba out before you go to bed."*

*"You don't need to remind me every time you leave the house, Pat. I'll let her out." Patrick paused at the doorway and looked back at his other half. She was still a lovely woman, even after fifteen years of marriage. Her honey blonde hair was always well coifed, her nails perfectly manicured and she had vivid, intelligent blue eyes which he had initially fallen in love with what seemed like a million years ago. Even ready for bed, she had a cold cream mask on her face and curlers in her hair in preparation for tomorrow.*

*"Cynthia, please don't neglect Jamba. She is getting older and her bladder can't handle holding it for long periods of time." Cynthia dropped the scarf she was working on and glared at him.*

*"Are you suggesting that I don't take care of your stupid dog? I always let her out, Patrick!"*

*Patrick held his ground.*

*"Last week when I came home from my conference, she had peed on the welcome rug. She never does anything like that unless she hasn't been out. I'm just asking you to remember, that's all." Cynthia sat forward rigidly in the bed, incensed.*

*"Well maybe something's wrong with her because I'm always letting her out when you're away. And if you don't trust me to do it, then hire someone to do it for you, you ungrateful boor! I take darn good care of that useless animal even though I didn't want her. But you didn't seem to care and brought her home anyway. Now I'm not babysitting properly for you. You are insufferable, Patrick. You better go before I say something I regret." Biting his lip, Patrick heeded her advice and left the house, fuming.*

*He was at the venue housing the bachelor party in fifteen minutes. The groomsmen had chosen a quaint lakeside tavern for the party. It promised to be low key and well behaved but Patrick was still shaking with anger when he walked inside. He tried to stuff his emotions under a superficial smile and greeted the other party goers. But he couldn't get to the bar fast enough where he ordered his first scotch.*

*Two hours had gone by and Patrick had really no recount of where the time had escaped but around ten thirty p.m. he was chatting to a mysterious sloe eyed beauty in a dimly lit corner of the restaurant. Her luxuriant black hair caught the candlelight like magic flecks and while later Patrick could not recall what they had discussed, he remembered wanting to hear her speak so he could listen to her mellifluous, throaty voice. An hour later, the groom had approached him to gently question how he was getting home and Patrick was apparently sitting very close to the ethereal beauty in the booth, still drinking scotch (at least he was told the following day).*

*By this point he had turned off his phone to avoid Cynthia's texts and phone calls.*

*Midnight found Patrick with the exotic stranger in the bathroom in a very compromising position. Two of the groomsmen had walked in on the act and quickly exited, waiting for Patrick to come out of the washroom so they could drive him home. He was barely coherent from the amount of alcohol he had consumed. They quietly unlocked his front door and gently pushed him into the house, awkwardly dressed and falling down. Neither of the men had wanted to explain to Mrs. Dean how her husband had come to be in such a state or be forced to answer any questions. The only certainty Patrick had at that point was that Jamba had not been let out for she urinated all over his feet as soon as he stumbled into the house.*

*The following morning, the entire town's phone lines were afire. It was too juicy a scandal to ignore. Pastor Pat was drunk and cheating on his wife with a stranger in front of members of his own parish? He was an instant outcast. He didn't even have time to beg Cynthia for forgiveness. By the time he had slept off the alcohol, he was staring at her emptied closet and dresser drawers.*

## Down South

Patrick snapped out of his reverie of mortification and glanced at his watch. Sarah Jane would be expecting him and Jamba very shortly.

"Come on, girl," he said to the pooch and they hurried out of the cottage down the road. As they neared the bushes, Patrick heard screaming. He and Jamba paused mid-step and listened. The shrieking continued from Sarah Jane's house. He began to run toward the commotion. Tearing around the corner, there was a crash and Damien threw open the screen and took off like the devil himself was on his heels. Tears streaked his face and he was wailing high and feral but he had disappeared before Patrick could react. When he looked back at the house, Sarah Jane stood on the threshold looking defeated. She tried to force a smile as she saw him but failed. Tears misted her incredible eyes as she waved for them to enter.

"I'm sorry y'all had to see that," she said, tiredly as she shooed them into her small home. "Damien has good days and bad ones. This ain't been the best one."

"We can do this another day. Please go deal with your son," Patrick said, gently. Sarah Jane shook her head.

"Oh no! I been slavin' away over a hot stove all day. Y'all gonna stay and eat. Damien will be back when he calms down some. Dontcha worry. It happens all the time. It's one of the reasons I decided to move all the way out ta here. Ain't no one to witness his breakdowns. In Baton Rouge, ma neighbors done be callin' the police an' Child Services on me once a week. No one understands what it's like." Her normally bright eyes were clouded with sadness.

"If you don't mind me asking, have you taken him to a doctor?"

Sarah Jane gestured for him to sit down at a modest kitchen table done in solid pine. She laughed mirthlessly.

"Yessir. An' all of them want to put him on this drug an' that drug. I even had him try some of them. Turned him into a zombie or robot or somethin'. Ain't no way for a child to live. So I keep him home an' school him here but I ain't the most educated woman but when I think of the alternative, I might as well lock him up in an asylum." She choked on her last words and sobbed. Her hand flew to her mouth as she tried to stifle the raw emotion she was feeling. Patrick was instantly at her side, embracing her. She stiffened at his unexpected touch and he backed away immediately.

"Oh, I'm so sorry! I didn't mean to – "

"No no! It ain't you, Patrick. It's...I ain't really had much male companionship since Damien's daddy up and left. I know you were just bein' supportive. I'm sorry I'm such poor company." They grinned sheepishly at one another and sat at the table.

"The gumbo's just simmerin'. Would you like a beer or glass of wine? Actually, I think I even have some of ma pa's moonshine in the cellar." Patrick shook his head quickly.

"No, no thank you. Just water will be fine." Sarah Jane's smile widened further.

"Not much of a drinkin' man?" she asked as she went to the small fridge and retrieved a pitcher of lemon water.

"No," he replied simply.

## Upstate
### *One Year Prior*

*"That was a wonderful service, Pastor Pat! I hope you and Cynthia will join us for brunch today" The Bransons were smiling hopefully at him and his instinct was to decline but Cynthia was pinching his arm ruthlessly.*

*"We would be honored to join you, Joe! Thank you so much for your continued support and Lana, your brownies were the biggest hit at the bake sale yesterday! I think you singlehandedly made our goal happen!" Cynthia cut in, beaming. "What can we bring?"*

*The couple and Cynthia continued to chat and Patrick wandered off toward the playground. The Bransons had invited them to brunch every single Sunday since Patrick had become Pastor and he had always managed to avoid their invites.*

*"It's awful manners, Patrick! You must think of what the members of this parish do for our church. Next time they ask us, you better accept!" Cynthia had warned him just before the service that morning. Patrick had merely nodded but he had no intention of doing what she suggested. Of course Cynthia knew that and had made it a point to be at his side afterward. He was beginning to find himself irritated with his wife over the tiniest issues. But he had found a way to cope with her annoying habits. As he watched the children playing happily on the monkey bars, he forced his mind out of the spot where it always went and circled back to the rear entrance of the church. The fire door was open and he slipped inside, unnoticed. He made his way to his office and secured the door behind him. Then he dropped tiredly into the high back leather chair and unlocked the bottom drawer to his desk. He pulled open the mickey of vodka and took a huge swig. He paused for a moment and after the burning sensation in his throat passed, he helped himself to one more before replacing the bottle and popping cough drop into his mouth. Well at least there would be mimosas at brunch.*

### **<u>Down South</u>**

Sarah Jane had not exaggerated her culinary talents; the gumbo was phenomenal. She had even set up a bowl for Jamba which the dog inhaled in three bites and begged for seconds. As Sarah Jane had anticipated, Damien did reappear before dinner was through. He ignored both of the adults and sat on the floor to play with Jamba who relished the attention.

"So do ya do fer a livin', Patrick?" Sarah Jane inevitably asked. Patrick considered lying but there was something about this woman that made him want to only speak in truths.

"I was a pastor but I'm not really doing anything at the moment," he responded, looking down at his bowl. Sarah Jane's face seemed to light up like a Christmas tree.

"Y'all must be really smart then!" she exclaimed. Patrick laughed.

"Well I wouldn't go that far!"

"Y'all gone to college, ain't ya?" Patrick nodded.

"Would y'all be willin' ta help me with schoolin' Damien? I ain't so good in English an' history an' artsy stuff. I kin hold ma own in math and science but spellin' dang if I don't go messin' everythin' up!" Patrick was taken aback by the offer.

"Well, I..."

"Oh, I kin pay ya! I'm a researcher actually. I do online consultin' for some huge firms so money ain't really a problem."

"I would be happy to help you with Damien," Patrick responded. "If Damien would be willing to have me. Damien, would you mind if I come and help with some of your lessons?"

The child looked completely startled at being addressed. He stared at Patrick with hole boring black eyes and then, after what seemed like an eternity, he shrugged, barely nodded and turned back to Jamba.

"Well I guess it's settled then! When do we start?"

The following morning, Patrick woke to contractors on the roof. The pale morning light was sparkling through the trees and despite his sore back from sleeping on the rough wood pallet in one of the two bedrooms, he felt elated for the first time in as long as he could remember. Even Jamba seemed contented as she followed him to the outhouse. He walked down toward the water, keeping a watchful eye out for alligators and splashed some cool water on his face before retreating back to the cottage. He dug a pair of jeans and a t-shirt out of the suitcase and quickly changed before leaving the construction crew and heading to meet Sarah Jane and Damien. He thought about the developmentally challenged little boy and wondered about Sarah Jane's husband. He wondered if a father would have changed the child's life substantially. He angrily pondered what kind of man would abandon a boy who needed more support than the average child and leave the mother alone to contend with the aftermath. Then he thought about Cynthia.

### <u>Upstate</u>

### <u>*Fifteen Years Prior*</u>

*"Are you happy, Patrick?" she asked as they drove home from the cabin. She seemed annoyed at having spent part of their honeymoon in the swamp but she didn't say anything out loud.*

*"Of course I'm happy! I've married my queen, we're starting our lives together upstate where we'll have a gaggle of babies and we are going to live happily ever after! How could I be anything but ecstatic? How about you? Any regrets yet?" He grinned teasingly at her and Cynthia flashed him a brief smile.*

*"Of course I am!" She turned to watch the gorgeous scenery. "Patrick?"*

*"Yes, my love?"*

*"I need to tell you something."*

*"You can tell me anything. I am your husband." He grinned wider as he said the word. He loved the way it sounded. "Husband. I like the sound of that. I wonder if I'm going to like the sound of 'daddy' as much. Probably. I guess we'll find out."*

*"Patrick, I had an accident when I was young, I fell off a horse," Cynthia said quietly. "And the doctor's have told me that I can't have children."*

### <u>*Ten Years Prior*</u>

*His head was pounding. He hadn't had a migraine since his late teens but the air pressure was affecting his blood pressure and he was suffering terribly.*

*"Cyndi? Cynthia?" he croaked from the bedroom but there was no answer. Only Jamba lay on the pillow beside him, nuzzling his neck. "Cyndi?"*

*She must have gone out while I was sleeping, he thought. The thought of getting out of the bed was agonizing but he had no choice. He slowly and painfully rose to his feet, trying to move as gingerly as possibly. The nausea was overwhelming but he needed to take some Aspirin before the pain got much worse or else he would end up hospitalized. Slowly, he shuffled into the bathroom and tried to remember where Cynthia kept the pain medication. He was unaccustomed to taking any form of medicine. He began rummaging through drawers when the cabinet in the bathroom produced no results. He found himself in Cynthia's beauty products when his hand closed around a circular package. When he looked down at it, he thought the pain had affected his vision but the logical, educated side of him knew what he was staring at birth control pills. His wife had been taking birth control pills.*

### *Five Years Prior*

*The party was in full swing and while everyone was having a grand old time, Patrick had one of his now trademark headaches. He looked around everywhere for Cynthia but he couldn't find her. Finally, he escaped to the backyard for some fresh air and snuck around to the side of the house. What he saw made his blood run cold; Cynthia was passionately kissing a man he considered to be one of his best friends. And Patrick slowly backed away and never mentioned the scene to anyone.*

## Down South

When Patrick appeared at the door, Damien actually smiled at him for the first time and he felt his heart swell. He realized that the child was more likely smiling at Jamba but Patrick still took it as a positive sign. The boy allowed them into the house and led them to a sunroom in the rear of the house. Sarah Jane was waiting for them there with coffee and fresh fruit for breakfast. The room was designed to be an educational but stimulating environment. The windows overlooked the bayou and all of the day creatures were peeking out of their hiding spots for the day. A black and white board were set up as to not obstruct the stunning view. Sarah Jane had already laid out the lessons for the day and Damien took his seat in an old style school desk. They started with a basic math lesson and Patrick was pleased to see how quickly Damien finished his assignments. The child had a natural knack for math and science. *Just like his mother*, Patrick thought with appreciation. He was warmed as he saw the interaction between mother and son. While Damien was non-verbal, the managed to communicate through gestures and he genuinely seemed to hang on to her every word. When it came Patrick's time to take stage, he began with one of his sermons, one that young Austin had liked so much, David and Goliath. He noted happily that Damien was enraptured by the story and afterward they took a break for lunch.

Damien took his tuna fish sandwiches outside to share with Jamba while Sarah Jane and Patrick sat in the cozy kitchen and talked. To Patrick's surprise, he found himself opening up to her about Cynthia, things he had never shared with anyone. She in turn talked about Damien's father and they both felt a deep connection to one another through the strangers they had married. They talked about their spouses openly.

"Damien's daddy was neva any good at facin' problems," Sarah Jane said. "I guess I shoulda seen that before we got hitched. He drank like a fish and got inta all kinds of bar fights but I was all struck by them big ole black eyes and them pretty white teeth. As soon as he realized Damien wasn't like other boys, he hightailed it outta town lickity split. Neva heard a word from him in ova five years now. Ain't no big loss. Damien an' I always did okay together."

"Even after I discovered that Cynthia had been lying to me on so many levels, I still wanted to be a good husband to her. I really did love her. Or at least the woman I believed she was. Aside from that one horrible, stupid night, I was never unfaithful to her. I never even considered it."

They smiled at each other and Patrick reached across the table to put his hand over hers.

"We do the best we can given what we got," Sarah Jane told him, giving his palm a gentle squeeze.

"And remember that God won't ever throw anything at us we can't handle," Patrick replied.

The days were long and wonderful, filled with lessons for Damien and walks through the swampland. The contractors finished the cabin and there was finally a bathroom, electricity and running water within its walls. Even Jamba was thriving in her new environment, attempting to befriend the racoons and once even a gator. The nights were less and less lonely, spent playing Monopoly with Damien and Sarah Jane. When the boy would go to bed, Sarah Jane and Patrick would talk until the wee hours of the morning, listening to the fish splashing in the water and the crickets chirping. They never seemed to run out of subjects to discuss. Sarah Jane was worldly and intelligent and a wonderful conversationalist. Once in a while they would drive into town and see a film at the small outdoor theater or go for ice cream. Sarah Jane and Patrick would stroll arm in arm and sometimes, Patrick would feel a small hand slip into his for a moment or two and then Damien would run off to be with Jamba.

One morning, a courier pulled up on the dirt road outside of the cabin just as Patrick was leaving for Sarah Jane's house. His heart in his throat, Patrick opened the screen and accepted the registered letter. A bittersweet feeling overwhelmed him as he tore open the envelope. It was the final divorce decree, signed by Cynthia. He put the paper back in the casing and slowly made his way up the road. When Sarah Jane opened the door, she noticed his serious expression.

"What's wrong?"

"I got my final divorce papers today."

A smile lit up her entire face.

"Ya don't say! So did I!" She reached out to a coffee table and produced a letter of her own.

"Jus' after y'all got here, I decided to start lookin' for Damien's daddy to end this charade once and fer all. I found 'im and I had him served with papers! Don't God act in mysterious ways sometimes?" Patrick felt all of his doubts disappear. He grabbed Sarah Jane by the waist, brushed her dark hair from her blue eyes and beamed down at her lovingly.

"I love you, Sarah Jane," he whispered. Then he leaned in and gently placed a sweet kiss upon her lips.

"Pa...pa...pa...!" They both turned to look at Damien who had appeared in the doorway to the kitchen, pointing at Patrick.

"Oh! Damien is trying to say my name!" he almost yelled and quickly threw his hand over his mouth worried about startling the boy. Sarah Jane smiled dreamily at him.

"No, honey. I think he's trying to call you 'pa.' Will you be my boy's pa?"

And Patrick could not remember a time when his heart had been so full, his life so complete. *Thank you, lord, for giving me another chance at happiness.*

"Only if his mother will agree to be my wife."

# MOTHER ANGEL

## NIKKI CARLSON

"Mama! Mama!"

She was at the crib, leaning down over the inconsolable child, her hands gently stroking the damp tendrils of hair, curls that were soaked in sweat from night terrors.

"Shhh...mama's here. Don't cry, mama's here," Vivienne whispered, reluctant to pick up the baby even though every fiber of maternal instinct begged her to lean over and do so. "Go back to sleep now, sweetheart. It's time to sleep."

The little one continued to wail, small chubby arms reaching up, big, brown eyes swimming in tears.

"Shhh....shhh....shhh..."

The door to the nursery opened and Ryan hurried in, half asleep with red-rimmed eyes and an unshaven face. She could smell stale whiskey on him as he slipped into the room and she wrinkled her nose in disgust. He reached past Vivienne and scooped Lily into his arms. Vivienne was completely surprised by his presence.

"Mama!" Lily screamed. "Mama! Mama!"

"Ryan! Put her down! She'll never learn to self-soothe if you pick her up every time she cries!"

"Daddy's here, baby. Shhh...don't cry. Daddy's here," Ryan cooed, turning his back on his wife and putting the sobbing girl to his chest, bouncing her slightly.

"Mama! Mama! Mama!"

"Ryan! Put her back in the crib!" Vivienne demanded, angry he was ignoring her. What is he even doing in here in the middle of the night? This is a first!

"Mama!" Lily was inconsolable. "Mama!"

As Ryan walked out of the room he began to rock Lily, leaving Vivienne staring after him.

"Ryan!"

"I know, baby. I want your mama too," he whispered to her soothingly.

Vivienne blinked and stepped after her husband but as she looked down to ensure there were no toys obstructing her path, she didn't make out her legs. Slowly, her eyes traveled up her body from where her feet were supposed to be and she suddenly realized that there was nothing there. Whirling abruptly, she turned to look at the full-length wooden mirror next to the change table. There was no one there. She did not exist. I'm having a nightmare, she concluded.

"It's not a nightmare," the faun whispered in her ear. "You're dead."

Rain-like droplets of sunlight fell through the maple leaves. The smell of wood burning filtered through chimneys and Vivienne felt both nostalgic and borderline euphoric as the comfortable and familiar scents of autumn filled the air. It was her favorite time of year, the fall. She continued down the street, pushing the stroller before her. Soon enough it would be Lily's first birthday and all of the fun of toddler-hood would begin. The incessant babbling and the toothbrushes in the toilet, the temper tantrums and the endless test of wills. The new mother looked lovingly down at her dark haired, sleeping angel and smiled. But for now, Lily was a still a small, vulnerable infant who needed her protection and she intended to relish this stage for the blessing it was. As Vivienne turned the corner, her small smile of contentment faded. Ryan was home already. She steeled herself inwardly as she slowly made her way up the front walkway with Lily. The child was beginning to stir from her nap and Vivienne groaned inwardly. The baby's timing for waking could not have been more off.

"Hi?" she called upon entry. "Are you home?"

"Yeah, babe, in the kitchen," came Ryan's response from the rear of the house. Taking her time, Vivienne unwrapped her daughter from the carriage and cradled her gently as the child became aware of her surroundings. Inevitably, Lily began to wail. Vivienne felt herself cringe. Ryan poked his head around the corner and scowled.

"What's wrong?" he asked sourly. "Why is she crying?"

Vivienne swallowed her anger and forced herself to answer calmly. "She's six months old. That's what she does."

Ryan grimaced but did not bother to respond and returned to the kitchen, leaving his wife to console the waking baby. Vivienne followed him into the kitchen and began preparing a bottle, carefully cradling Lily in one arm. Ryan did not offer his assistance as he sat at the island, biting into a sandwich he had just prepared.

"You're home awful early," Vivienne commented, popping the nipple of the warm bottle into her daughter's mouth. Eagerly, Lily accepted it, instantly silencing her wails.

"Yeah, they're calling for rain this afternoon. All the contractors went home," Ryan answered. "What did you do today?"

"Lil and I just got back from a walk. We went swimming this morning. I cleaned up a bit while she took her nap."

Ryan raised an eyebrow and looked around the room skeptically but he made no comment. Vivienne felt her temper flare. How dare you! You have no idea what it's like to be home with a baby all day long! You have no idea how much work I put in! She thought furiously. But she said none of these things. Instead, she took Lily into the living room and placed her in her playpen as she suckled on her lunch. She turned on the television and found a nursery rhyme channel to entertain her daughter before turning to pick up the toys strewn about the floor.

"What time is dinner tonight? My mom is asking." Ryan appeared in the doorway, holding his cell and looking down at a text message. Vivienne blinked trying to recall what day of the week it was.

"Why is she asking?" she asked slowly. Ryan frowned angrily.

"My mom and Jamie are coming for dinner tonight. We planned this last week!"

Vivienne felt her blood pressure rise to an almost dangerous level. She had no recollection of making the arrangements. That doesn't mean I didn't agree to it, she conceded silently. It only meant that she had probably forgotten in the midst of the chaos that her life had become. The thought of not only cooking for her mother-in-law and her mother in law's new boyfriend but having to actually entertain them for an evening was insurmountable. Lily had still not learned how to sleep through the night so Vivienne was functioning on minimal sleep over and above the day to day trials and tribulations of child rearing. Of course, Ryan could not be bothered to ever get up with the baby during the night. That's not fair. Ryan works really hard. And Lily needs her mom right now. It will get better. It will just take time, Vivienne tried to reassure herself.

"Six o'clock," Vivienne told him.

Vivienne spun her non-existent body around to stare at the creature. She immediately noticed the horns atop his deer-like head, slightly taller than the two velvet ears poking out of his bald skull. As her gaze lowered, she noticed his forehead sloped eerily between wide, innocent eyes. It was the eyes which captivated Vivienne as they were no definitive color. They were gold, green, brown and purple but somehow uniform. Staring at them was making her lightheaded and somehow queasy. She continued to look past his lopsided smile and down his naked chest to his waist where two horse legs supported his lean body. Vivienne swallowed.

"Are you the devil?" she whispered fearfully. The half smile became an unsightly mess of cracked, yellow teeth as his chapped lips parted and he let out a howl of laughter.

"Oh! It never gets any less amusing! No matter how many times I get asked! The devil! Ah, you mortals are so unimaginative." Vivienne didn't know how to respond. She waited but in spite of the shock she had just received, she found herself staring at the doorway wistfully after her family. She suddenly recognized she was no longer standing in Lily's nursery but instead in a vast nothingness. She stood, invisibly with the faun, uncomprehendingly. The beast began to circle around her, half predatory, half soothingly, his long index finger extended, touching the area which would have been her face...if she actually existed. His deep, strange eyes fixated on her.

"No, sweet child," he cooed mockingly, "I am not the devil. I am your friend. Your one and only friend." Vivienne felt a chill at the words but she maintained her silence and waited. He continued to do the slow dance around her, sizing her up as if she were some lamb for the slaughter.

"You and I will become very familiar with one another," he continued. "We have plenty of time to get to know one another. Plenty of time."

Vivienne decidedly did not like his tone.

"I do not want to become familiar with you!" she snapped. "What am I doing here?"

The faun found her words humorous and began to laugh again. Abruptly he stopped, his unpleasant grin fading.

"You don't have a choice, child," he snarled. "You are bound to me..."

He paused a moment, his eyes sparkling with something sinister. "Unless you can find a way out."

Before Vivienne could question what he meant, he disappeared and she was enveloped in the emptiness.

The shrieks of laughter resounded through the neighborhood. Someone had released a bright purple balloon into the air and Vivienne watched as it floated into the almost cloudless sky. The winter had melted away into a glorious springtime and she couldn't have hand picked a better day for Lily's first birthday. Her nieces and nephews ran amok through the backyard among the other children, high off sugar and adrenaline. The bouncy castle was filled almost to capacity and Vivienne hurried over to shoo some children out lest the structure collapse from the weight. Ryan's mother stopped her as she passed her spot in the sun. Vivienne rolled her eyes behind her dark sunglasses.

She tried to prepare herself for whatever gem her mother in law was going to deliver.

"Dear, I hope you put some sunscreen on Lily. It's warming up quite quickly," she said to Vivienne in that condescending voice which made Vivienne want to strangle her. Vivienne arched an eyebrow. Is this woman serious? She asked herself.

"Gillian, it's sixty degrees," she replied. "It's hardly sunscreen weather."

Gillian shook her head as if to say "you don't know anything" and smiled sardonically.

"It's not the heat which will harm her skin, Vivienne. It's the UV rays. UV rays are – "

"I know what UV rays are, Gillian!" Vivienne said more sharply than she intended. "I will get some sunscreen."

"Oh? Are you sure you have some? I looked for some in Lily's room but I didn't see any. I can have Jonathan go to the store and pick some up." Vivienne followed her mother-in-law's gaze to her latest conquest, a man barely older than her own son. The younger woman couldn't resist the opportunity.

"Oh, no need to trouble Jamie. I have some in the bathroom. I try not to keep poison in the baby's bedroom." She watched as Gillian's eyes flashed with annoyance.

"You mean Jonathan," she replied flatly.

"Oh...what did I say?"

"Jamie."

"Oh, whoops...I guess I got confused...with all the...'J' names," Vivienne answered lamely. Inwardly she was giggling. Her mother in law's borderline promiscuity was a poorly kept family secret. Her momentary win was deflated a second later, however, when Ryan appeared with Lily in tow. She was bawling at the top of her lungs, face red and tears streaking her cheeks. Ryan roughly shoved the child into Vivienne's instinctively outstretched arms.

"What happened?" Vivienne asked, scooping up her daughter. Ryan shrugged.

"I have no idea! She babbled something at me and then started freaking out when I didn't react. I don't speak baby talk. You figure it out." Vivienne gritted her teeth and wiped Lily's tears from her face. I guess I'm going to have to, aren't I? she thought angrily.

"Shhh...what happened baby?" she asked the child. "What do you need?"

"Mama!" Lily wailed. "Mama!"

Gillian shook her head and snorted.

"You are spoiling that child," she said above Lily's cries. "You shouldn't coddle her when she's being a brat. In my day, we'd get a wooden spoon for behavior like this."

"In your day they didn't have Children's Services," Vivienne replied, bouncing Lily in her arms. She would not be calmed. In fact, her wailing got louder. Ryan was getting irritated by the noise.

"Lily! Enough!" Ryan yelled, glaring at the baby. Giving Ryan a scathing look, Vivienne spun on her heel and walked away from mother and son, worried she was about to say something she would regret the rest of her life. As they disappeared into the sanctuary of the house, away from the noise and relations, Vivienne had a daunting thought. If anything ever happens to me, this is who Lily will be stuck with to raise her.

"Mama! Mama! Mama!"

Vivienne watched helplessly as her daughter sat up in the crib, sobbing out her name. She had been crying for what seemed like hours but in reality, it probably had not been more than a few minutes. Still, Ryan had no responded to her.

"Ryan! For heaven's sake! Lily is crying!" she heard herself yell into the darkness. For a brief second, Lily's voice faltered and the baby turned her head upward to where Vivienne hovered.

"Mama?" she whispered.

"Hi, baby!" Vivienne felt invisible tears form in her eyes. "Can you see me? Can you hear me?"

Her dark eyes peered searchingly into the void, rosebud lips parting. Then she let out a feral moan so heart wrenching, Vivienne swore that she felt herself die all over again. The doorway flew open and Ryan ran in, tripping over the Persian rug. Picking himself up, he ran toward the crib.

"Lily! Lily are you all right?" He rushed to pick up the distraught child. "What happened? Are you hurt?"

He looked her over as he rocked, making shushing noises.

"Mama!" she screamed over and over. "Mama!"

Looking completely defeated, Ryan clung to the small body, murmuring softly. Another form appeared in the doorway.

"What is going on? Why is she screaming?" Gillian demanded.

"It's okay, mom. She had a bad dream. Go back to bed," Ryan answered without turning to face his mother.

"Well, it's difficult to sleep with a caterwauling child in the next room, Ryan," Gillian retorted, stepping into the nursery. "Give her to me."

Vivienne watched in anger as her husband handed over their child.

"Now, Lily, listen to grandma," Gillian began in her usual no-nonsense manner. "It is time to sleep." Of course, the toddler was far too distressed to heed any reasoning and her cries escalated. She looked at her father in desperation.

"Daddy! Mama! Mama! Mama!" she continued to screech. Ryan turned his head away so he wouldn't have to look at his daughter's anguish. Vivienne was appalled.

"Your daughter needs you! What are you doing?" she howled at her husband.

"Lily! That is enough crying. You will go to sleep now," Gillian stated firmly. She put the troubled child back into the crib.

"Mom! She's still crying. You can't – "

"It's for her own good. She has to get used to the fact that her mother is gone, Ryan. Now go to your room. She will cry herself to sleep." Gillian pushed her son gently through the threshold and closed the door behind her. Vivienne stood frozen in absolute disbelief for a moment. *Did that just happen? Did they just leave my child, hysterical and bereaved alone in the dark?* Beside her, the faun chuckled.

"This is why we will be friends for a long, long while," he reiterated, looking at his long, bony hands. Vivienne spun to address him.

"We are not friends now," she hissed, turning toward Lily's crib, determined not to be perturbed by the being. "Why would you assume we would be friends for any amount of time?"

Again the faun laughed.

"Ah, sweet child. You aren't listening to me. I am the only friend you have. I am the only friend you will ever have again at this rate." Vivienne felt a stab of fear despite her resolve not to be intimidated. She tried to touch Lily's saline soaked cheek but of course, the act was useless. There were no fingers to make contact.

"Why is that? Is this what usually happens to everyone after they pass on? Is this purgatory?" The faun looked irritated with the barrage of questions.

"How sheltered of a mortal were you that you ask such ludicrous questions? What is usual? What is purgatory? These are only words without sustenance."

Vivienne was about to ignore the faun but her fighting spirit in her would not let it go.

"I may be sheltered but at least I don't speak in a cryptic riddle. I have the decency to explain myself, especially when I can see someone might benefit from some clarity." Those multi-colored, enigmatic eyes sparked with both appreciation and annoyance. When he offered a smile this time, Vivienne instantly regretted her words.

"You will understand when you understand. There is nothing I can say to offer comfort to your plight. But I can tell you this; you should get used to my companionship because the way I see it, you're bound to be stuck here for eternity. And I'm the only one who can see you!"

I can't do this anymore. Vivienne stared listlessly out the bay window of the front room, watching the sun shower without actually seeing the drops tease the thirsty leaves on the front lawn. Lily was watching Sesame Street and flipping through a hard paged storybook of princesses on the hardwood floor. Every once in a while, a sweet giggle would escape her throat and Vivienne would abandon her reverie to smile automatically as their eyes met. This isn't fair to Lily. This isn't fair to me. I just can't live like this. The revelation had come the previous night as Ryan had come home from work. Lily had just begun winding down for bath time when he walked through the door, covered in drywall dust and paint.

"Daddy!" Lily yelled, jumping up from the sofa to embrace her father.

"Hiya, baby! How is my favorite girl?"

"Daddy!" she yelled again. Her vocabulary was growing every day but sentences had yet to come. Vivienne smiled at the exchange. She was, without a doubt, becoming daddy's little girl. Ryan ruffled Lily's hair affectionately and stood up to kick off his shoes.

"Daddy brought you a present," he told her, smiling. Vivienne's smile faded as Ryan reached into his pocket.

"Ryan..." she warned as he pulled a chocolate bar out of his pocket. "It's almost seven o'clock."

"Chakit!" Lily howled happily. "Chakit!"

Ryan shrugged and grinned.

"You can't say no now, mama," he laughed, unwrapping the candy and pulling off a gooey piece.

"Ryan, just a little tiny bit – "But it was already too late. Lily was scarfing down sugar like it was being outlawed. Vivienne frowned but did not say anything. Ryan saw so little of Lily with his late work hours. She knew that the chocolate was his way of bonding and apologizing simultaneously. Vivienne didn't necessarily approve but she certainly wasn't about to infringe on their father/daughter time. After fifteen minutes of wrestling around on the floor, Vivienne laughingly announced bath and bed time for Lily. A slight protest ensued but Vivienne hustled her small daughter upstairs and into bed. It took well over an hour to put Lily to sleep with the fresh amount of glucose in her blood stream. When Vivienne had finally made it back to the main floor, Ryan was asleep in the recliner, still in his work clothes. And Vivienne realized he had barely acknowledged her presence since he had arrived home. It hit her like a flood. They hadn't been intimate in months, not even a kiss good-bye in the mornings. He slept on the couch almost every night and at first she had justified it as exhaustion but the more she thought about it, the more she saw all the signs that her marriage had burnt out. Now it was only a matter of who would actually say the words.

"Mama! Daddy!" Lily announced, rising unsteadily to her feet and pointing at the front door. "Daddy!"

Vivienne realized her daughter was right; Ryan was home already. It was not even three o'clock and the day was clear. She felt a smidgen of alarm. She slipped off the loveseat to join her daughter at the front door. A moment later, Gillian strolled in, Ryan on her heels.

"Gamma!" Lily cried hugging her grandmother. "Daddy!"

Vivienne blinked, the feeling of foreboding growing in her stomach.

"Hello, angel!" Gillian called, leaning down to kiss the small cheek before her. "Hello Viv. How are you?"

"Gillian, what are you doing here?" In her surprise, Vivienne heard her rudeness after the words left her lips. Her mother in law's smile thinned.

"Nice to see you too, dear," she said, ignoring the slight. "I am here to watch my angel."

Vivienne looked behind her at Ryan for an explanation. From behind his back, Ryan pulled out a bouquet of light pink baby roses. Stunned, she accepted them, still not understanding.

"We're going out tonight, Viv," Ryan said simply, ushering his mother into the house.

"Why – I mean what's the occasion?" she responded, dumbfounded. For a sickening moment, she wondered if it was their anniversary and she had forgotten. Ryan smiled sadly and embraced her.

"The occasion is you are my wife and I appreciate how you hold this family together. And I know I don't tell you this enough but I love you very much." Vivienne felt her heart swell up with hope and she looked into his husband's sheepish eyes.

"I love you, Ryan," she replied. Lily clapped her hands gleefully and clamored to be picked up.

Gillian reached down to scoop up the child.

"Oh, by the way, I just started seeing someone so I hope you don't mind if Philip stops by this evening after Lily is in bed," she told them.

"Mama!"

Vivienne was finding it hard to bear watching this night after night. Ryan had stopped coming in during the wee hours, allowing Gillian to take over completely. Every night, Gillian would come in, lecture Lily gently and leave her to cry herself into an exhausted slumber. Some nights Vivienne would try to sing and talk to her young daughter but after that one time, her words had no effect on the toddler.

"Ugh, please cease that racket!" the faun snarled as Vivienne paced the room singing, waiting for Lily to fall asleep. "You sound worse than the child."

"You don't have to be here," she shot back. "In fact, I insist, please go!"

The faun growled. "I don't have the option. Someone needs to keep an eye on you."

"Says who?" Vivienne circled the crib, hoping her movement would catch Lily's attention and help alleviate her agony. "You already said I am stuck in this limbo forever. Why do you need to be here? Surely you must have other places you'd rather be."

"That, sweet child, is the understatement of the millennia. There are hundreds of places, no, thousands of places I would rather be but at this time, you and I are bound. There is only one way for me to leave." Curiosity got the best of Vivienne and against her better judgment, she voiced her question.

"How do I get rid of you then?"

He smiled that awful leer.

"I can only leave if you do leave first."

Vivienne turned to stare at him.

"What – "

Gillian finally threw the door open to the nursery stopping Vivienne in mid-sentence. She looked angry.

"Lily!" she snapped. "Lily, you must stop crying!"

"Gamma! Mama! Mama! Mama!"

"Lily, your mama is not coming back. You must learn to accept that." Vivienne was horrified at her mother in law's tone.

"Gillian, she's not even two years old!" Vivienne screamed. For a second, Gillian seemed to freeze. Her crown of dyed red hair lifted to the direction of where Vivienne stood with the faun.

"Do you hear me, Gillian?" Vivienne tried again. Gillian's pupils dilated and she slowly backed away from the crib. A shiver seemed to crawl down her spine and she shuddered.

"Sleep, Lily. Go to sleep," she mumbled, hurrying out the door and firmly closing the door so hard, it was almost a slam. Vivienne turned to the faun.

"She heard me," she said to the faun in surprise. He shrugged nonchalantly.

"It happens sometimes. It's rare with older mortals as they are conditioned by the poisons of your world and lose touch with their natural instincts. When your daughter's grief lessens, she too will be able to sense you but right now she is overpowered by emotion. She is also too young to understand her surroundings properly. It would have been better for her if you had died when she was four or five." Vivienne smirked.

"I'll keep that in mind for next time I die," she answered facetiously. The faun shrugged again. Lily was beginning to tire and Vivienne looked longingly at her as her swollen eyes began to close. She would give anything to be able to hold that small, warm body against hers just one more time, even for a short minute. She continued pacing the room again.

"I beg of you, cease all the movement! You're making me queasy," the faun growled.

"Do you immortals get queasy?" she quipped.

"I imagine it's a very similar feeling to nausea which you are giving me."

Vivienne sighed. "What would you have me do instead?"

"I find it odd that you haven't visited your husband," the faun commented blatantly. "Is that because you blame him?"

Vivienne stopped her laps of the room. He was right. She had not once gone to visit Ryan. She had not seen him but for the few times, he had come to check on Lily. Do I blame him? Should I blame him?

Vivienne could not remember the last time she and Ryan had sat down over a meal and conversed. They had a lovely dinner at La Piazza over candlelight and wine and talked about everything they had neglected discussing over the past two years. After dinner, Ryan took her dancing to a new Latin club. It had been years since they had gone salsa dancing and Vivienne felt ten years younger. They shared kisses on the dance floor like they were teenagers and danced with wild abandon. It was two o'clock in the morning when the stumbled out of the sweaty venue, drunk, giggling and very much in love once more. Then Ryan reached for his car keys and Vivienne immediately shook her head.

"No. We'll take a cab home. We can pick up the car tomorrow." He argued that he was fine to drive and headed to the car. Vivienne had paused, reluctant to make a scene when the night had gone so perfectly. They had rekindled their faltering romance in one amazing shot, just at a point when she was ready to call it quits. Was it worth throwing it all away over this? They may never get another shot to make things right. She watched as Ryan fumbled to get the key into the door of the Toyota and made her decision.

Driving home, she stared quietly out the window, the streetlights whizzing by and counting the blocks. Home was not far away when he ran the stop sign. She saw it happen in slow motion. The red hexagon zipped by and as she turned to call out in protest, the truck barrelled down on the taxi cab. A split second before impact, Vivienne saw their Toyota which was slightly ahead, turn onto their street. Ryan was home safe. And then there was blackness.

She crossed the threshold to their bedroom and was immediately overwhelmed by the stench of dirty laundry and old whiskey. There were piles of clothes on every item of furniture. The bed itself had been stripped of all its linens and in the center of the bed lay her husband, passed out drunk. Anger colored her sight. How dare he drink after what had happened? How dare he leave Lily to cry while he slept peacefully? In her fury, Vivienne desperately wished she could kick him. Instead, she crawled into the bed beside him.

"Ryan!" she yelled. The faun guffawed but her husband did not stir. Irritated, she lay beside him and stared at the ceiling.

"Viv! Viv I'm sorry! Viv! Please, Viv!" At once, the words flew out of Ryan's mouth in a torrent. Vivienne turned to him. He was talking in his sleep. "Viv, don't get in the cab! Please, Viv! Don't get in the cab!"

Vivienne felt sorrow wash through her as she watched her husband began to toss and turn. Sweat appeared on his brow.

"Viv, I'm sorry! Viv, please don't get in the cab!" Thrashing violently, his cries were getting louder. "Viv! Viv! Viv! Viv!"

As his voice reached a feverish pitch, the door flew open again and Gillian hurried in. She rushed to the side of the bed and shook her son violently.

"Ryan! Ryan wake up!" she yelled. He began to stir out of his nightmare, still calling out for his deceased wife. Slowly, bloodshot eyes opening, he became aware of his surroundings.

"Was I talking in my sleep?" he mumbled at Gillian. She nodded, stepping back.

"Sorry, mom," he said, sitting up. "It's the dream. It's always the same dream. Why didn't I go with her, mom? Why didn't I listen to her?"

Gillian did not answer and turned to leave the room. But as she did, Vivienne was shocked to see her mother in law's eyes full of brimming tears. She almost ran out and Vivienne realized it was so her son would not see her cry.

"Mama! Mama! Mama!" Vivienne lay on the floor under the window in Lily's room. The faun was sprawled out lewdly beside her, not by design but simply by the very nature of his being. She had given up on singing or talking to Lily. She saw the futility in those actions now She had succumbed to the helplessness of her circumstances and now allowed the depression to overcome her. She was waiting for Gillian's customary cold arrival and soon, Lily's grandmother appeared. This was only the first time that Lily had woken so far that night. This night, however, Gillian leaned over and picked up the child.

"Shhh.... grandma's here, angel. Grandma's here." Surprised by the turn of events, Vivienne sat up and watched as Gillian took her granddaughter to the rocker and lulled her back to sleep. Vivienne slowly walked over to her and watched as Lily nodded off.

"I know you're here, Vivienne," Gillian said simply. "I can feel you."

Vivienne was at a loss for words so she said nothing.

"We all miss you terribly. I'm sure you can see that. We're trying our best to get by without you. I know you think we're doing it all wrong," she continued in a quiet voice.

"You are!" Vivienne replied. She thought Gillian smiled but it was difficult to tell in the darkness.

"You can go, dear. Everyone will be okay. I will always be here for Ryan and Lily. And they have each other."

"Go where, you stupid old woman?" Vivienne yelled. "I don't need your useless advice. I need you to take care of my daughter properly!"

The faun cackled hysterically.

"You shut up!" she told him furiously. He laughed more loudly.

"Go now, Vivienne," Gillian said again. She rose out of the chair and gently laid Lily in the crib. "I promise, everything will be okay."

"Crazy old bat," Vivienne muttered as Gillian left the nursery. "She abandons my baby most nights, my husband is passed out drunk, completely ignoring Lily, the house is a pig sty. Oh yeah, if I had somewhere to go, I'd run right out of here!"

"Did it ever occur to you that maybe their world won't fall apart without you?" the faun asked casually. Vivienne whipped her eyes around to glare at him.

"Have you been here these past weeks? They can barely keep themselves alive, let alone Lily!"

"I suppose they are very fortunate that you are here then," the faun replied slyly. Suddenly Vivienne understood his point. There was nothing she could do to help them now. The only thing that would make them whole would be if she returned to them and of course, that could not happen. She blinked at looked at the faun with sadness as this realization settled.

"Will they be okay?" she asked, suddenly, hoping that he would give her the absolution she so desperately needed. He shrugged his characteristic shrug and grinned.

"It appears that the only one not alive is you so statistically speaking, they are already in better shape – well from a mortal standpoint." Vivienne chuckled in spite of herself and for the first time, she shared a smile with the creature. He really wasn't so bad. Lily began to stir in her bed. Vivienne felt tears well up in her eyes. This was never going to get easier to watch. She could not do this forever. Lily let out a cry and Vivienne turned to look out the window at the black night. In the distance, she saw something shimmering, like a mirage. It shone shimmery silver but Vivienne could not make out what it was exactly. Lily's cries began. Vivienne began her usual pacing routine, trying to tune out the distress. Time will heal her pain. She will grow up and be happy and healthy and never think about me. It's a blessing she's so young. She will recover from this faster. She will be okay. Ryan will be okay. She and Ryan will have an amazing relationship. Vivienne was at the window again. The mirage was closer now, just beyond the neighbor's backyard, a floating orb of light. Staring at it made Vivienne feel calm in spite of Lily's crying.

"Do you see that?" she asked the faun, pointing out the window. But the faun's face had changed. His horns had retracted into his skull and he was only a smooth, bald head with two soft ears on a deer-like face. His eyes had taken on more of a gold sheen than silver now but they were still filled with all the colors. His lips were no longer cracked but supple and shiny and he smiled, beautiful, ivory and genuine with no sign of the previously held leer. He wore a white gown over his once bare chest and Vivienne noticed the tunic was the same shimmery glow as the light outside the window. She suddenly felt very light, floaty even. The faun nodded and reached out a hand to her. His gnarly knuckles were now soft, callous free fingers and she accepted his touch even though she did not exist. His palm warmed her to the core of her being.

"Are you ready?" he asked her, softly. Lily sat up in her crib, tears flowing free. Vivienne looked at her daughter's sad, anguished face and then at the faun. She was conflicted, almost afraid. Would she ever see her baby girl again?

"I don't know..." Vivienne whispered.

"You must be sure," the faun told her. "You can't come back to this place once you let go." Vivienne stared at Lily, searching her face for any sign that her daughter needed her to stay at her side. Please, Lily, give mama a sign, she silently begged her daughter. I will stay here forever if you want me to do that but I need to know. Send me a sign. Anything.

"Daddy! Daddy! Daddy!" Lily called through her tears. And Vivienne knew then that she was ready to move on. Lily had her daddy. She nodded at the faun through her own stinging eyes and they watched as the orb of light slipped through the walls of the nursery and toward them. The faun gently squeezed Vivienne's hand and together, they stepped into the shimmering glow of eternity.

# LONE MOON RANCH

FAITH DUNLAP

PART ONE

She felt a mix of relief and despair as she watched the Boston skyline fade away. She felt a mix of relief and despair. She knew she would never come back to her beloved hometown. There was nothing left for her there. In fact, all she had left fit into a small carry-on bag. Her life had shattered, and most of the pieces had blown away in the wind.

She grabbed her phone and read Colt's email again.

*I am a simple man. I own the Lone Moon Ranch in Helena, Montana. I've lived here all my life. I am 26 now. I am looking for a wife, someone who can take over the household duties; cooking, cleaning and such. Also, to assist with various chores around the ranch. I need someone who is not deterred by early mornings and not afraid of hard work. In return, I will make sure you are well-taken care of. I am seeking a partner, not a companion. Please contact me if you have questions.*

He didn't include a photo and she never asked for one. It didn't matter what he looked like. She appreciated the fact that he sounded very businesslike in his email. That's what this was – a business deal. She had placed an ad on a mail order bride site - not for love, but for security. Colt fit the bill. He needed a wife and she needed an escape. Of course, he had no clue what she was escaping from. She hadn't been completely honest with him about her past.

She tossed her phone back into her purse. She rubbed her thumb against her ring finger as she laid back against her seat and closed her eyes. She didn't want to think about Nick. But he was always there, lurking just below the surface. She could picture his dark eyes and dangerous smile. When they met, he made her feel alive and invincible.

Loving Nick was like grabbing hold of a lightning bolt. He had lit her up and then burned her to ashes.

They got married a month after their first date. Nick was wild and impulsive that way, and she couldn't deny him anything. But Nick was also a drunk and a gambler. He got so wasted on their wedding night that he passed out in the hotel lobby. Three months in, he had blown through all her savings. He became violent and erratic when the money ran out. He isolated her from her family and her friends so she had no one to help her. And she couldn't leave him. They were each other's obsession even though he scared her. But then one night he crashed into another car and almost killed the driver. She could picture his face the day of sentencing. Six years. And the way he looked at her the last time she went to visit him, to tell him she had filed for divorce. She lied to him and told him it was all his fault. But she couldn't lie to herself. She knew she was just as much to blame. Maybe he struck the match but they had both danced within the flames.

Their 2-year marriage had stripped her of everything. She lost her condo, her car, and even her job. Her parents had both passed way, and both her brother and sister had given up on her. She needed to start over. And there were worst ways to do that than a beautiful ranch in Montana. So, she bought a plane ticket and a new dress using the only credit card she had left and swore to do her very best to not look back.

***

Colt Malone stood inside Helena Regional Airport. He jiggled his truck keys impatiently against his thigh. Joelle's flight had been delayed. And while he was many things, patient was not one of them. It was a trait that had never come easily to him. Mainly because he rarely liked to be idle.

Nearly every woman that walked past him, smiled. Women had always noticed him. But it had been a long time since one had shared his life or his bed. Not since Ashlyn. They had grown up together. He chased her from the moment he was big enough to run. He couldn't recall a moment of his life that he didn't love her. She had been his best friend and then his lover. But Ashlyn wanted to chase something of her own. Her dreams had taken her far from Montana and far from him. She was in California now. He used to think they'd get married and build a life together. He used to think love matter more than anything. Now he knew better. Love broke you in ways that would never heal. And he didn't intend to ever give someone that kind of power over him again.

He made the ranch his whole life. His father had died three years prior, and he had no other family. When his father died, the ranch and all the responsibility of it became his. It was a huge undertaking. The ranch was financially in bad shape. It was burden his father had never shared with him, but something he inherited just the same.

Things still weren't great. He worked from sun up to sun down, but the ranch was still in jeopardy. He had to lay off most of the staff. He had taken out new loans to pay off old ones. But the ranch was still in debt. He knew he didn't have time to be angry but he was. He was angry that his father hadn't been a better businessman. He was angry at his mother for leaving when he was young. He was angry at the hand life and love had dealt him.

He couldn't say what came over him the night he went online and found the mail order bride website. He guessed it was his loneliness. He wanted to come home to a hot meal and a warm body. He didn't want someone to fall in love with but he did want a partner. Someone to share his burdens and his life. Joelle's ad had stood out to him. She was beautiful but haunted. Long, dark hair and big expressive eyes. She looked like a painting from another time and place. She seemed like a woman that could possess a man and make him beg at her feet, and yet gave him the sense that she didn't want to possess anyone. What she wanted was security. A place in the world that belonged to her. He could give her that, even if he could never give her his heart.

The gate opened, and a rush of people came toward him. Cole scanned the crowd looking for her. He had looked at her picture a dozen times. He had stared into her hazel eyes and memorized the color of her lips and the curve of her neck. His finger had traced each wave of her long, raven hair. But that picture had in no way prepared him for the real-life version.

He called her name and she walked toward him, her cheeks flush and her hair slightly tangled. She was smiling, but it didn't quite reach her eyes.

"Colt?"

"Hello," he said. His voice came out slightly gruff.

"Hi." She hesitated for a moment, but then sat down her bag and leaned into him.

He didn't think, he just put his arms around her and closed his eyes. He felt his whole body respond to hers, full and warm against him. She smelled of a lavender and citrus. And when she pulled back to look up at him, he felt breathless for the first time in a long time. Yep, she could awaken a hunger in a man and he was in no way immune; and it was a hunger he had almost forgotten was there. His pulse quickened, and this animal desire to ravage her was stirring inside. He swallowed, and took a long, shaky breath.

"I'm glad I'm here," she said softly.

"So am I."

They stood for a moment, still half in each other's arm. He took another breath and steadied himself.

"We should get going Do you have more bags?" he asked.

She smiled again in a sad sort of way. He saw something in her eyes for the briefest of moments, but then it was gone.

"This is all I have." She gestured toward the bag at her feet. "I meant it when I said I was looking forward to a fresh start."

He picked up the bag for her. "My trucks just outside then," he said. "We have an appointment at the courthouse in less than an hour."

She nodded. They had done the paperwork online, and obtain their marriage license. He had told her he didn't see any reason to put things off, and so he made an appointment at the courthouse for them to be married that afternoon. She didn't seem to want to wait either.

They exited the airport and Joelle's breath hitched as she took in the landscape. The blue sky was cloudless and seemed to have no end. The land before them was flat and rugged until your eyes found the mountains jutting into the heavens.

"It's so beautiful," she said softly.

"It is," he agreed. He had never strayed far from home. The soul of him came from the land and those mountains.

They reached his pickup truck, and he tossed her bag into the bed of it. The truck was painted a fire engine red and it was well loved and taken care of.

"After you." He opened the passenger side door, and then without thinking he reached down and touched her cheek. This made her lips part slightly.

An invitation?

Her lips were as red as his truck and he couldn't seem to look away. Slowly he bent down, letting his own lips graze her's. His hands fell to her waist, and he pulled her body to his. He kissed her, tasting the sweetness of her. She didn't respond to him at first. But he felt the exact moment when she let go. She molded herself to him, and her body hummed. She made a sexy, breathy sound and it about did him in. Somehow he knew she had the same kind of demons that he did. She buried things too. Maybe like him, she still held out hope that one day she'd find redemption.

She pulled away first. She stared at him, her breath ragged.

"Colt, I didn't come here to fall for you."

Trying to regain his composure he said, "I didn't bring you here to fall in love."

"Before we do this, I need you to promise me again. Love is not part of the agreement."

"I do. And I'll keep my promise." He nodded toward the open truck door and ran his fingers through his hair. She was holding his gaze, searching.

"So will I," she said and got up into the truck. They were on the road a moment later, heading for the courthouse on the other side of town.

***

Joelle tried to stop her hands from shaking. She and Colt had arrived at the courthouse, and she could hear the Judge and Colt talking. But all she could think of was that moment she spotted him in the airport. He had on a pair of Wrangler's that fit him well and a button-down shirt. Cowboy boots of course and she had spotted a matching cowboy hat in the truck. He was also sporting a five o'clock shadow even though it was only noon. He wore it well. Too well. He was quite possibly the most handsome man she had even laid eyes on. His auburn hair that curled at the ends and those smoky eyes rimmed with lashes that went on for days. And when he kissed her...

"We're ready." Colt touched her arm lightly. The Judge was just beside him.

"But are you ready my dear?" he asked. He had a soft voice and a kindly face.

"I do – I mean I am," she stammered. They both smiled at her and she laughed nervously. Colt had her undone and that was not part of the plan.

The simple ceremony took less than ten minutes. When it concluded, Colt leaned in and kissed her again. This kiss was softer and sweeter. It held a promise instead of passion. It told her he would be there and he would take care of her.

"Let's go home," he said.

It was a good twenty minutes before they reached the ranch. Colt turned down a rocky drive. Lone Moon Ranch sat a mile off the main road with rolling hills on either side. The main house was average in size, painted red with a white a trim. A barn sat directly to the left of the house, and acres of pasture and field to the right. She breathed in the smell of cut grass and watched as hundreds of dandelions danced in the late afternoon breeze. She spotted several cows in the pasture, and could make out the sound of horses nearby.

He put the car in park right in front of the house. He got out and came around to open the door for her. They stood in the driveway for a long time in silence. He was letting her take everything in. She had never seen so much land and beauty in all her life. She felt like she had been dropped in the middle of nowhere, and the middle of nowhere looked a lot like paradise.

"Hello!" A middle-aged woman came down the front porch steps. She was drying her hands on the apron she wore. Her graying hair was pulled back into a tight bun, and she had a big smile on her face. She came toward Joelle, and pulled her into a tight hug.

"My goodness, you are gorgeous." She pulled back, holding Joelle at arm's length. Then she leaned in and hugged her again. "We are so happy to have you. And congratulations to you both!" She turned to him then, and he bent so she could kiss his cheek. She looked at him with such affection that it made Joelle smile.

"This is Minnie," Colt said. "Minnie, this is Joelle."

"You can call me Jo."

Minnie turned back and hugged her again.

"Minnie is a dear friend," he explained. "She comes by once or twice a week to help tidy up or cook one of her delicious meals. I don't deserve her at all, but I honestly don't know what I would do without her."

"Oh shush." She slapped him playfully on the arm. "I love you like my own son. And how I wish I could do more for you, love." Her eyes got misty. "But here you are now." She turned back to Joelle. "I am just so happy that Colt has found someone to love again."

Colt cleared his throat uncomfortably and she got the impression that Minnie had no idea how they had met. And maybe she would be a bit taken aback if she knew he had basically gone online and ordered up a bride.

"Well, I am happy to be here. So happy," Joelle said. "Colt has just stolen my heart and I don't ever want it back."

Minnie clapped her hands in delight, smiling brightly at them. He was giving her a look, and she gave him a sideways smile.

"Well, come on in. You must be tired and famished. I have dinner all ready." She directed them inside, like a shepherd herding her flock.

Once inside the house, she took a moment to look around her new home. All the rooms were big and open, with high ceilings and lots of windows. The living room was to her left, and a large stone fireplace stood against the back wall. He didn't have a whole lot of furniture, a leather couch, and two big chairs.

She made her way to the kitchen, which was also airy and full of lots of natural light. A large island sat in the center and a small breakfast nook in the corner. The dining room sat off to the right, and both rooms blended well together.

"There's a roast warming in the oven. And biscuits on the table," Minnie said. "You've outdone yourself again," he told her.

"Oh, don't fuss on me. You sit down and enjoy your dinner. I'll be around tomorrow, Jo, to help you settle in."

"Thank you – so much," she said.

Minnie smiled and touched her cheek. "You're going to be very happy here," she promised and then she was gone.

He glanced toward the dining room table. "Shall we?" he asked.

She nodded, her stomach rumbling at the thought. She hadn't eaten breakfast or lunch that day. In fact, she hadn't eaten much at all lately. Certainly, nothing that resembled a home cooked meal.

They ate in silence for several minutes. She savored the biscuits dipped in honey. She glanced up at him, the late afternoon sun poured in through a window, and she could see the flecks of red in his hair.

"I'm sorry you didn't have any family or friends here today," he said.

"I don't have a family. None that speak to me anyway. And no real friends either," she told him. "It's just me."

"Why doesn't your family speak to you?" he asked.

She looked up, meeting his gaze. "My parents died last year. It was a car accident. That sent my spiraling a bit. I didn't always make the best decisions. My brother and sister are both older than me. I guess they handle things better than I do. She has two kids and he owns his own business. I'm the black sheep and they finally threw in the towel."

"Doesn't seem fair," he said. "You're family. They shouldn't just turn their backs on you."

"I don't blame them," she replied honestly. "I hurt them a lot. They felt like they needed to protect themselves."

He sat back in his chair, holding her gaze across the table. "Is that why you left? Why you married me?"

"I don't have anything, Colt. I'm embarrassed to say that, but it's the truth. But now I'm your wife. And here we are together, and I want this to work. I want this ranch to be as much mine as it is yours. I want us to take care of it together."

"And you mean that?"

"I do."

"You know, it's just me, too. Sure – I have friends. Wonderful friends. But no family. This ranch is all I have, and I work every day to hold on to it for me... For us." He paused still watching her. "And I'm sorry about your parents. I never knew my mother, but my daddy passed away three years ago. So, I mean it – I am sorry."

"It's been over a year. You would think it would hurt a little less by now."

"It won't ever hurt any less. You just learn to live with it."

They took their time finishing dinner. She liked talking to him and he seemed to like to listen. She talked a lot about Boston. It was her first love after all. They also talked about the ranch, and she asked him questions about his life growing up.

When they finished, he stood and pushed his chair back heavily. "I get up at five. We should go to bed."

Bed?

His eyes had turned to smolder. Slowly, she stood as well.

"Okay."

"Jo, listen - I've never had a woman in my bed who didn't want to be there," he began. "But it's been a long time. So, I am hoping you will join me in it tonight." With that, he stepped around the table and walked past her. She listened to the echo of his boots as he went upstairs.

She felt rooted in place for several seconds, twisting her dinner napkin back and forth in her hands. The attraction she felt toward him was undeniable. And even hours later, she could still remember the taste of his lips on hers. A slight tremor went through her at the memory. It had been a long time for her as well. And he was her husband...

He was sitting on the bed in the first bedroom. There was a large bay window to the left with a window seat. The setting sun painted the room a dusty rose color.

"I don't sleep in the master bedroom," he explained. He watched her as she scanned the bedroom, taking it all in.

"Why?" she asked softly.

"It's not mine. Never was, and I don't see how it could ever be. Is that a problem?"

She shook her head no. She was still standing in the doorway, and they watched each other across the room. She could see his chest rise and fall with each breath. He seemed to be tracing her whole body with his eyes.

"Come to bed," he told her. His voice was a husky whisper.

Again, a tremor went through her. She felt an ache and longing deep inside. She had not just been alone; she had been lonely. And she had been that way long before Nick got arrested.

"Colt." She came to him, straddling his waist and pushing him down on the bed. She leaned over, creating a canopy with her hair. It blocked out the world, so all that was left was the two of them. They held on to each other. Some moments thrashing against the night and all the loneliness that had held them captive. They were iron and lace, colliding in moments of raw, insatiable need. And in other moments, they were soft and gentle and warm like a summer breeze. Their bodies lifting and swaying like waves to the shore.

PART TWO

Joelle rolled over in bed, pulling the covers around her. She opened her eyes to see that the sun was making its way across the sky. She sighed happily. Her whole body felt sated and relaxed. She smiled, thinking of the night before. She could feel her insides vibrate and stir. She wasn't sure any man had ever made her feel that way. She was literally humming from the inside out. She was more than satisfied, yet the hunger for him lingered.

"Jo."

She jumped slightly, then turned back over in bed. Colt was standing over her, completely dressed. He was clean shaven and he smelled wonderful. She reached out, her hand caressing his.

"Come back to bed," she told him.

"Back to bed?" he repeated. "You need to get up."

She blinked and sat up. She wasn't dressed, so she pulled the sheet up around her.

"What's wrong?"

"There's no breakfast made. And I am heading out. There is housework to be done. I thought we discussed all this."

"Colt..."

"I need a partner, Jo."

"I know that." She blinked several more times, pushing back tears that suddenly burned her eyes. "We were partners last night," she said softly.

"I have to start my day. I'll eat some biscuits left over from last night. But I'll be back at noon, and I'd like something hot waiting for me." He turned then and stalked out of the bedroom.

She smacks away a few tears that had managed to escape. She got out of bed, pulling the sheet along with her. She needed a shower and she needed coffee. And she needed to get herself in check. She couldn't lay in bed daydreaming about him all day. He was a business decision, nothing more.

She padded down the hall, the floor cold against her bare feet. Her clothes were still in her suitcase which she'd left in the foyer. The house was silent as she made her way carefully down the winding staircase. Just as she reached the landing, the front door swung open.

A man stood there looking like John Wayne come back to life. He was most likely in his forties. But a life working under the sun had leathered his skin, and it made him appear older.

"Well, I beg your pardon," he said. He respectfully glanced away as she clutched the sheet tighter.

"Who are you?" she asked.

"Jeff Loggings, darling," he said. "You must be Joelle."

"Good morning." Minnie came through the door but stopped in her tracks when she saw Joelle. "Goodness, Jeff." She slapped his arm. "We're sorry to barge in, honey. Go on up and get yourself ready. It looks like you had a wonderful wedding night." She gave Joelle a wink, and then pushed Jeff toward the kitchen.

She grabbed her suitcase and ran back up the stairs. She was out of the shower and dressed in ten minutes. As she headed back downstairs, the smell of perked coffee wafting up to her.

"I hope you don't mind, I got things started," Jeff said, nodding toward the coffee pot.

"Not at all. Thank you." He handed her a steaming cup. Minnie was bustling around, going back and forth between the refrigerator and the pantry.

"How are you settling in?" Jeff asked as they sat down at the table.

"Just fine."

"Is that so?" Jeff gave her a look that remaindered her of her father.

"I slept in," she admitted. She glanced at the clock hanging on the wall. It was a quarter after seven.

"Getting up at dawn takes getting used to. You'll get into the swing of it. Minnie, Colt and I have been doing it our whole lives. I wouldn't know how to sleep in even if I could."

"I could teach you," she said with a smile.

He returned it. "Don't let him scare you off," he said a moment later.

"Scare me off?"

"Colt is certainly rough around the edges. But beneath all that there is a heart of gold. He's just been lonely too long. And he feels the weight of the world on his shoulders. When his daddy died, it about did him in. That was all the family he had, and he was just here one day and gone the next. I don't think Colt even realizes how much it affected him. How much it broke his heart."

She took a long sip from her cup. She certainly knew about heartbreak.

"He doesn't scare me a bit," she said. "I'm quite fond of him." She was surprised to hear some truth in her words.

Jeff leaned across the table and said quietly, "I know how you met. Minnie doesn't. God don't tell her! But I know. And I know Colt told you he wasn't looking for love."

"He did. I'm not looking for love either," she confessed.

"Is that so? Now, darling, everyone is looking for love. Surely, you know that."

"I've had love."

"And how did that work out?"

"Lousy," she replied. "So lousy that it turned me off to the prospect altogether."

Jeff laughed. He had a genuine twinkle in his eye. "If I had a nickel for every time someone said those words. For every time I said those words."

"But aren't you and Minnie married?" she asked.

"Yes. Third time for me, though. I was pretty bitter on love, but there it was all these years – right in front of my face." He stood up then, draining the last of his coffee.

"Minnie, I am heading out," he called. She was just coming out of the pantry. She came over and kissed his cheek. "It was nice meeting you, Jo."

"It was very nice to meet you, too," she told him.

"I'll see you soon." He put on his hat and tipped it toward her. Then he headed out the back door.

***

Minnie stayed for a few hours. She started a pot of chili, and she showed her around the house. It was almost noon when she left, promising to be back the next day. Joelle started a load of laundry and put some cornbread in the oven. It was ready twenty minutes later when Colt came in.

"Smells good," he said.

"Wash up," she told him.

She gave her a tired smile, and memories of the night before flooded her again. She felt her cheeks go warm and her body go flush as he brushed past her. He stood at the kitchen sink for several minutes, washing away the morning. When he finally sat back down, she placed a hot bowl of chili in front of him.

"I have to go into town this afternoon," he said. He turned to his chili and downed half the bowl in a matter of seconds.

"Should I come?" she asked.

"No need. I have an appointment at the bank. I'm a little behind on the mortgage."

She looked up at him. "What do you mean?"

"My daddy was a great man, but his finances were a mess when he died. I've been working day and night to get things in order again. But times are hard."

She dropped her spoon into her bowl. Bits of chili splashed across the table. "I don't understand. I thought you owned this ranch."

"The bank owns the ranch, Jo."

"But you said you could take care of a wife." She didn't know why she suddenly felt so panicky, but she did.

"I can. The manager is a buddy of mine. Everything will be alright," he said. "I'm doing my best. I've been running uphill for three years now."

"I don't know what to say." And she didn't.

"Listen, I apologize if what I said made you believe I owned this ranch right out. I don't. But I hope to someday. I can tell you this, I will always take care of you. But this isn't a prison, it's a marriage. You can leave anytime you want if this isn't what you want."

"Do you want me to leave?"

"No – I don't."

"I just – I can't go back." Tears burned her eyes. She couldn't look up at him. But she heard him push his chair back and come around the table.

"Then don't." He reached down and tilted her head back so she was looking at him. Then he bent and kissed her lips, softly at first and then harder. He pulled her up from the chair and against him. She wanted him. Wanted him right then and there.

As if reading her mind, he lifted her up and onto the table. He came down on top of her, the weight of him making her whole body ache with want. She arched into him and he moaned softly, his breath warm against her ear. And when he took her, she clung to him as if she was lost at sea and he was the only thing keeping her from drowning completely.

***

Colt left the bank feeling uneasy. He was almost three months behind on the mortgage. Not to mention the taxes were due. He had one month to catch up on payments or the ranch will be put up for auction. He hadn't a clue how he would manage, but he was certainly going to try. He just had to work harder. He knew how to do that.

He spent the next few weeks doing just that and showing Joelle the ins and outs of ranch life. She was able to help with some of the manual labor, but not much. He was simply stronger and had been doing it his whole life. There was always hay to cut, bale and stack. Always a fence that needed mending or manure to haul. Joelle helped with other things. She worked a lot in the garden and with the animals. She seemed to enjoy the animals more than anything, especially the horses. He liked watching her with them. In fact, over the next few days, he caught himself watching her more and more.

He also liked coming home to her – most days. It had become painfully obvious she had never kept house before. She could cook - sure, but nothing from scratch. And she tried baking but burned practically everything. She told him that she cleaned every day. He was sure she did. But it was more like tidying up here and there. She had yet to give the whole ranch the good scrubbing that it needed. It was gnawing at him. They had fought about it more than once.

"I just don't know what you want from me!" she told him.

"You know exactly what I want, Jo. Come on."

"A housemaid."

"A partner! Don't act like I don't work myself into an early grave. Is it so much to ask to have a clean house and a decent dinner?"

She stormed out of the room. He found her an hour later, listening to music in the living room. It was a slow song, something country and twangy. The sun had gone down, and the living room was in shadows. He held out his hand to her, and she took it. They swayed together to the music.

"I am trying," she said sadly.

"I know." He held her, getting lost in the moment.

They went upstairs a little later. This is what he longed for all day. It didn't matter if they had bickered all day, he couldn't wait to get under the blankets with her each night. She was beautiful and soft. She awakened things in him that had been dormant for too long. In those moments, he could care less if she knew how to bake bread or use a vacuum. He was completely under her spell.

***

Joelle sat drinking her third cup of coffee. It was late in the day. Colt would be home soon. A part of her hummed with the anticipation of seeing him. The other part of her worried. She glanced around the kitchen and dining room, searching for some spot she hadn't dusted or dish she hadn't washed. She knew he was disappointed. She was not a housewife. At least not one that lived up to his standards. But she was trying. She was becoming more and more aware of how hard she was trying. How much she wanted to make him happy. That made her nervous. There were days when all she thought about was the moment he would walk through the door.

"Hey," he came in just then. He looked rugged and handsome, tired from a long day. "Something smells sweet."

"I baked a cheesecake today," she said proudly. "And I didn't burn it."

"I didn't know you had to actually bake a cheesecake."

"Exactly," she replied. They both smiled.

He sat down, mail in his hand. He began to shuffle through it as she got up to make him a sandwich.

"Jo, why would a lawyer be writing to you?" he questioned.

She stopped mid-step and turned back toward him. "What?"

He held up one of the envelopes and gave her a questioning stare. "Well?"

"I don't know," she said. "Let me have it." She snatched it from her hand.

"What's going on?" he asked with a frown.

"I think it's just about some property I use to own," she lied.

He stood up and came toward her. "Then let's open it." His voice had gone cold.

"It's personal."

"You're my wife..."

"Colt, please."

"Is this about us, Joelle? What are you trying to do – what are you after?"

"After?" she repeated. "What does that mean?"

"Just open the envelope!"

"You think I trying to take something from you? After the past four weeks, that's what you think of me?"

"I don't know what to think. Just open it."

She threw the letter at him, hot tears springing up in her eyes. "This has nothing to do with you. It's about me. I was married before, Colt. He was a drunk and an abuser, and he's in prison now. And now you know."

He took a step back as if he'd been punched in the gut. "You were married before?"

"I was. He took everything I had. He gambled it away. He drank it away. He became violet when it all ran out. And he almost killed someone." Tears were streaming down her cheeks now. "I'm sorry I didn't tell you. I should have."

"Then, why didn't you?"

"A lot of reasons. Mostly because I didn't want you to know. I didn't think you'd want me if you knew, and I needed you to want me. And I was embarrassed. I had been such a fool for him. And it's hard to admit our mistakes sometimes..."

"You lied to me."

"I'm sorry."

"So am I." He turned and walked out the back door.

"Colt," she said. The tears were raging now. She sunk down on the kitchen tile and cried her eyes out.

PART THREE

Colt didn't sleep at all that night. He stayed downstairs on the couch. He could hear Jo above him, pacing the floor. He could hear when she cried. He wanted to go to her, but he couldn't. Finally, he got up and got in the shower. Joelle had finally fallen asleep, and he didn't wake her before he left. He drove into town. Ashlyn was coming to meet him.

He sat at a back table of the local diner. He and Ashlyn had come here almost every weekend when they were dating. He thought about how young and free they had been. He was still young, but he didn't feel very free anymore.

"Colt."

He looked up, and there she was. She looked just the same, if not more beautiful. He stood up as she fluttered into his arms. When they sat down, she reached across the table and held his hand.

"I've missed you," she said. "I heard you got married."

"I did," he replied with a sad smile.

"I'm happy for you. I mean that," she told him.

He nodded slowly. "I know you do."

"Do you love her?" she asked.

Did he?

He knew he had been falling for her more every day. It hadn't been his plan. But it had happened just the same.

"Love is hard," he said.

"It's not," she replied. "Not everyone runs from love, Colt. Not everyone is as big a fool as I am." She squeezed his hand and then let it go. She shuffled around in her purse and then pulled out an envelope. She slid it across the table.

"This should take care of things," she told him.

"I'll pay you back, I swear."

"I know," she said softly. "I am just glad I could help. I love that ranch. And your daddy would be real proud of you."

"Would he?"

"Believe me, he would. You've built a nice life for yourself. You should let yourself enjoy it."

He smiled at her across the table. "Maybe you're right. It meant a lot to see you, but I should go." He stood up, sliding the envelope into his pocket. He came to the table, bent down and kissed the top of her head. "Thank you."

She nodded, reaching up and taking his hand one more time. She held it for a moment and then let him go for good.

***

Colt had been gone all day. It was getting late, and Joelle was drained. She had packed a bag, and she planned on leaving in the morning. Her heart restricted at the thought. Despite her best efforts, she was falling for him. But the truth was out now, and he didn't want her anymore.

"Hi." Colt appeared in the doorway. "I want you to take a ride with me."

She didn't question him. She just got up and followed him outside. It was cold, and she shivered slightly. The world was dark, not even the moon was out as they headed for the barn. One of the horses was out, already saddled.

They rode for a long time without speaking. She felt like they were the only people left in the world. And when they reached a meadow, he got down off the horse and brought her with him. They sunk down in the cool grass, under the sable sky and made love. It was slow and sweet and tender. So much so that she felt like her heart might burst.

"Every day for the past month I have asked myself the same two questions," he said, lying beside her.

"And what are they?" she asked.

"What am I doing? What are we doing?"

"Come up with any answers?"

He gave her a sideways smile. "Some. But they terrify me."

"Why?"

"Because I'm falling in love with you. I broke my promise. And you lied."

"I'm sorry."

"I know. And I know why you did it. You deserve better than him. And I'm sorry for what he did to you." He reached over and took her hand.

"I didn't want to fall for you either. But I did. A little more every day. Colt – please understand. I didn't know how kind a man could be. And yes, you want things your way. Your stubborn and a perfectionist. And you work too hard. But you're also loving and compassionate. Strong and supportive." She turned to face him.

"Jo..."

"I fell for you, too." She had come here to escape love. But everything catches up to you eventually. No point is running. And she supposed she always knew deep down it would be a losing battle. The first time she saw him, she knew. The first time he kissed her, she knew. And when they made love...well, she certainly knew then.

"I promise never to keep anything from you again," she said.

"And I promise to take care of you every day of my life."

"And I promise to love you, Colt. And never leave you."

"I promise to love you and worship you." He kissed her softly. "This time, I'll keep my promises."

She smiled against his lips. "So will I."

THE END

# The Oath

Becky Coburn

**Chapter One**

Another day of doctoring.

Dan went into the medical field for all the wrong reasons. He excelled at science at a young age and his parents were both in the medical field. His whole life seemed to be pre-ordained. He would become a doctor like his father and wind up marrying a nurse just like dear old dad. He went to the right schools, attended a Lutheran college and would have an exotic dog (doesn't matter what kind, as long as it is purebred) named Abercrombie.

Dan would go onto do all of those things except get married. At the age of thirty-five, he remained single but definitely had his share of rolls in the hay. He had a nice house like his father did and had a St.Bernard waiting for him named Abercrombie.

Dan inherited all of those expectations from his parents. But what he didn't want was the dissatisfaction.

A dissatisfaction that grow larger by the day, just like the cancer in some of his patients.

Dan strolled into Maya's room with his clipboard in hand, reviewing the findings from her latest blood work. He smiled at the young woman. "Good morning, Maya," he said.

Maya sighed and managed a half smile for him. "What's so good about it?"

Dan frowned concernedly at her. "What seems to be the problem today?" It was their daily routine, and although Maya's supposed problems never seemed to manifest in fact, regardless of what types of readings they did, it was still his job to ask.

Maya gave half a shrug, looking as though a full shrug would be too much effort for her. "You know, the usual. Joint pain, stomach pain, nausea, and yet the nagging anxiety telling me that I need to do something productive today or else I'll really go crazy here in the hospital."

"Hmm," Dan flipped through the blood test results again. "Well, we've been able to rule out another few things with the latest set of blood work."

"Meaning, you still have no idea what I have," Maya said flatly.

"Like we said when we started this thing, it's probably just an infection. We'll continue to keep you here under observation for as long as you'd like, and of course we'll keep supplying you with antibiotics and painkillers as necessary."

"For as long as I'd like," Maya muttered darkly. "What you're really saying is that nothing is wrong, according to those papers that you have, and it's really just all in my head."

"Of course not," Dan sighed. "I'm just saying that whatever it is, we're going to do our best to beat it. You've been very strong these past few days."

"Thanks. I'm just glad to know that you're taking my case so seriously. Most other doctors don't believe that I'm telling the truth."

"But you'd have no reason to lie about medical issues," Dan gave her a winning smile to put her at ease. "Now, why don't you lie back and close your eyes, and I'll put another blast of painkillers into your IV drip?"

Maya nodded, closed her eyes and leaned back.

Dan went about his job with practiced precision and efficiency.

"I'll be back this afternoon to check on you again," he patted May on the arm. "But if you need anything, you know you can always call."

Dan exited Maya's room and caught the eye of Craig, walking down the hall with his eyes scanning over a clipboard.

Dan couldn't stand Craig.

Yet another person on the staff that he had to feign friendliness with.

"Morning," Craig said.

Dan wanted to give him one of Maya's 'what's so good about it?' but refrained.

"Craig," Dan said. "How you doing?"

Craig nodded toward Maya's door. How is she this morning anyways?"

"You know Maya," Dan raised his one of his eyebrows. "Every single morning, she acts like she's in so much pain that the world is ending. It's just a standard infection, and there's nothing else showing on any of the blood test we've tried. So she really has nothing to complain about. But that doesn't stop her…"

"They seem to always put you on with the difficult ones, eh?" he asked, shaking his head. "But I guess it's because you're still somehow able to charm their pants off, even when they're half-delirious with pain and drugged to the gills. I was in with Linda this morning, and she's still asking for you. I swear, she'll bake you a cake if she ever gets out of here, even though you've really had nothing to do with her healing process since she was first brought in."

"Chicks dig me, man," Dan said in a faux 1970s hippie accent.

"Umm, yeah."

"I think they give me the interesting cases so I won't be bored. ," Dan glanced back at his clipboard. "I need to go and check on Tracy. She gets worried that she's been forgotten about if I'm not there at 10am sharp. Have a good morning."

"You do the same."

Dan walked away from craig, holding his hand to his forehead, rubbing it as if he wanted to get the memory of Craig's existence out of his memory.

"Are you feeling all right, doctor?" a woman asked behind him.

Dan turned at the musical sound of the voice and stared in surprise at the woman standing there. Beautiful and blonde, he couldn't help but stare for a beat. Her blue eyes matched the color of her scrubs.

"No," he said in answer to her question. "No, I'm—I'm fine."

"Okay," the woman said slowly, as though uncertain. She held out her hand, though, a bright grin on her face. "I'm Paige, by the way. I'm new here; I don't think we've met yet."

"We haven't," Dan said confidently. If he'd met her already, he would definitely have remembered it. He couldn't have asked for a better fantasy than the gorgeous woman in front of him, dressed in her blue scrubs.

"Now is the part where you probably tell me your name.

Dan laughed, realizing that she was still standing there with her hand outstretched to him and that he was still gaping at her like an idiot. He quickly shook her hand. "Uh, I'm Doctor Smooth. But most people call me Dan."

She laughed. A good sign that he didn't totally blow it.

"Sorry to stare, we just normally don't get absolute angels like you around the ward here. It's a lot for the mind to take in with no notice."

Paige laughed again and shyly ducked her head. "Well, that's very nice of you to say." She paused. "Are you headed in to see a patient? It's my first day so they've told me to pick someone and shadow them, but I'm not sure how I'm supposed to pick someone when everyone's just running in different directions!"

Hell fucking yeah, Dan thought. One of the Gods above or whoever was in charge of the universe finally conspired something in his favor.

"You can definitely tag along with me for the day," he said. "Its going to be busy but you'll learn a lot."

"That's great," Paige enthused. She turned so she was walking in the same direction as him. "So tell me about your first patient."

"*Next* patient," Dan corrected, smiling to take the sting out of his words, though. "You'll get used to it, but everyone here comes on shift at different times, so even though you might be just starting your shift now, some of us have been on since late last night."

"Oh!" Paige said. "Of course, that makes sense. So tell me about your *next* patient."

## Chapter Two

The rest of Dan's shift was relatively easy. Mostly, he just had to check up on his various patients and make sure that they were as comfortable as they could be with their various illnesses. Paige was a perfect helper there, too: she fluffed pillows and smiled happily and generally charmed everyone just as well as Dan ever had.

Dan himself wasn't immune from her charms either. She had a winning smile and a cute little giggle that she let loose a couple times, and Dan couldn't help but wonder what she looked like when you stripped those scrubs off from her.

Of course, she was a good church-going girl, he quickly learned, so he expected he would probably have to take her to dinner first. But that was a small price to pay.

"Well," Dan said when they left the last of his patients, "that's about it for my shift. If you want, though, I can show you where the break room is and we can have a quick coffee before I leave you with someone else."

Paige smiled at him. "I'd like that," she said. She shook her head. "I don't know how you still have so much energy after all of that, at the end of your shift. But you're still just as kind and patient with all of them."

Dan shrugged nonchalantly, even though he was secretly pleased by her words. "It becomes habit after a while," he said.

"So it isn't genuine?" Paige asked, sounding disappointed.

Dan blinked and momentarily considered how to answer her. He doubted she would appreciate hearing his *real* thoughts on some of his patients. "It's not that it's not genuine," he lied, even though in most cases, it definitely was. "It's just that... You know how you act differently in public than you do in private? For me, it's kind of the same with my patients. There's a special brand of politeness that I have for them that isn't like the politeness I have in any other context. It's not a bad thing, it's just...the way it is."

The thing was, it was hard to be genuine when you were dealing with the same patients day after day, the same types of illnesses year after year... He would have needed the patience of a saint to get through years on the ward and still have a heart of gold. Instead, he acted charming enough around his patients and bitched about them to his colleagues as soon as he was out of the room. He wouldn't have been able to keep his sanity otherwise. He would have burnt out within a year.

"That makes sense," Paige said. She shook her head and grabbed two cups out of the cabinet so she could pour them each a cup of coffee.

"Anyway, enough about work; I'm off-shift," Dan said, flopping down on one of the chairs and waiting for her to bring him the coffee. "Tell me about yourself."

Paige giggled. "That's a pretty tall order," she said. "Let's see. I'm twenty-seven years old, just finished up my nursing degree and excited to get started here. I've always wanted to be a nurse, ever since I was a kid playing dress up. But I guess I never really realized how *long* it would take!"

Dan laughed along with her. "Yeah, but now you have the rest of your life to do what you love doing," he pointed out. "The study part was only a small portion of that time."

"True," Paige agreed, handing him a cup. Dan took a sip and was pleased to find that she had added a bit of cream without even asking. It was perfect.

"Tell me about yourself outside of work, though," he said. "What are your hobbies? What do you do on the weekends or in the evenings?"

Paige shook her head, sliding into the seat across from him. "Honestly, I've been studying for so long that I feel like I need to rediscover my interests," she confessed. "You know, for so many years now, it's just been classes and work and homework and studying and flashcards, and when I actually got a moment to myself, I usually only had the energy to order some takeout food and watch some crappy TV in the living room." She laughed, this time a little self-consciously. "I mean, don't get me wrong, I'm not a recluse or anything. I have friends, and I see them...well, as often as I can spare. But..."

"I'm a doctor," Dan reminded her. "I know what that's like."

Paige smiled. "Yeah," she said. "Sorry, I'm just used to having to justify things to everyone. Most people just don't understand. It's good to be around people who do. And everyone here is so *friendly*. The place where I did my internship, everyone was always too busy to be friendly, or the guys were only friendly because they were trying to get into my pants."

Dan shook his head. "Sounds pretty miserable," he said. "Are you from this area? Where did you go to school?"

"I'm not from here, no," Paige said. "I used to live in a little suburban town in Washington State, and I went to school up there. But I sent out applications to, like, a hundred places, just hoping that someone would hire me somewhere. And I'm excited to get to explore somewhere new—if I have enough free time to explore."

And that was exactly the sort of opening he was looking for... "Why don't I show you around a little?" Dan suggested. "I've lived around here my whole life, so you could say I'm kind of an expert. Are you working on Saturday?"

"No," Paige said. "I'm working today, tomorrow, and then not again until next Tuesday—Mary said she scheduled me that way so that I kind of get my feet wet this week but still have a bit of time to settle in before I really get to work. So I'm free all weekend."

"Excellent," Dan said. "There's a great little market that runs on Saturdays, so we can start there, do a bit of exploring around the city, and then I'll take you out to dinner at one of my favorite places that evening—how does that sound?"

"That sounds perfect, actually," Paige said. "Gosh, it's so nice to meet someone so friendly here. We're going to be great colleagues, I can already tell."

Dan smiled at her, keeping up the act. When she had properly fallen in love with him, he'd make his move. And then, as with many other women in the past, he would never call her again. If things got complicated around work, well. There were a half-dozen hospitals in the area, and with a bit of experience under her belt, she should have no trouble transferring.


**Chapter Three**

That Saturday, Paige showed up at their meeting point in a cute little yellow sundress, her long hair twisted into a snaking braid. Dan had expected her to look different outside of work, but he couldn't have expected how pretty she looked. He smiled at her and held out an arm. "Well, don't you clean up nicely," he said.

Paige giggled a little. "You too," she said, slipping her hand into the crook of his elbow and eyeing his jeans and flannel. "It's a pretty different look from those scrubs, that's for sure."

"Like what you see?" Dan asked.

Paige blinked and then gave an aborted shake of her head. "I'm ready to see some of the city," she said.

Dan frowned a little but then forced a smile. Maybe she was just shy. He'd need to be more tactful. But for now...

He steered her into the midst of the market stalls. "So they sell basically everything here," he told the woman. "Handicrafts, produce, you name it. When Girl Scout cookie season rolls around, they're always down here too. I do a lot of cooking, and this is one of the key stops along my route—but I got my shopping out of the way this morning, before we met up, so I won't bore you with all of that today."

Paige laughed. "I wouldn't have minded," she said. She gestured around at the stalls. "I just love how colorful it all is," she said.

Dan led her through the market. They paused at a few of the stalls as she examined different things, but for the most part, they meandered pretty cleanly through it. Then, he led her around the city a little bit, pointing out major landmarks and attractions. All the while, they kept up a light stream of chatter.

Dan thought everything was going well, but right before they reached the place he intended to take her for dinner, Paige got a call. She stared down at the screen, a frown on her face and then gave Dan an apologetic look. "You don't mind if I take this, do you? It's a friend."

"No problem," Dan said, even though it really was one of his big pet peeves when people weren't able to ignore their phones for an entire afternoon. He stood awkwardly to one side and tried not to listen to one side of Paige's conversation.

When she put her phone back in her pocket, though, she looked even more apologetic. "Sorry, I know you wanted to go to dinner, and I'm sure you know a really good place. But my friend is having kind of a crisis—she just broke up with her boyfriend because apparently he was cheating on her, that pig—and I think she needs me there. We've been friends for ages, and she's one of the only friends I have in this city, so..."

Dan wanted to scowl, but he knew she wouldn't appreciate that. Instead, he'd act like it didn't bother him, and they'd have an excuse to go to dinner another night soon. She'd remember today fondly, and his flexibility in letting her leave before dinner would earn him extra points in her book.

So he smiled magnanimously at her and nodded. "I totally understand," he told her, even though he really didn't at all. If he was out having a good time with someone and a friend called in need of moral support, well... He had to figure Paige's friend had other friends there in the city that she could call on. But that was fine. "Tell your friend I hope she feels better," he said, even though he really wasn't sure what to say.

"Thanks," Paige said. She smiled at him. "And don't worry—I will be going out for dinner with you some other time. This is just not the right time, I guess."

Dan pulled her into a hug, lightly kissing her cheek—but he had a feeling that was the most she would allow. "I'm sure I'll see you around work this week," he said. "But you have my number as well."

"I do," Paige agreed. She gave a quick wave. "Enjoy the rest of your evening, Dan!"

"You too, as much as you can," Dan said. He grinned crookedly. "Tell your friend whatever you have to, but remember that not all men are douchebags that sleep around!" It was kind of ironic coming from his mouth, but she didn't need to know that.

Paige laughed and hugged him again. "I'll remember that," she said. "See you around!"


**Chapter Four**

On Wednesday morning, Dan quite literally ran into Paige at work as he was coming around the corner. He opened his mouth to say something sharp to the other person about staying on the right side of the hallway, but when he saw it was Paige, he fortunately managed to put a smile on his face before she saw his scowl.

He caught her elbow, not because he thought she was actually going to fall but more because it gave him an excuse to touch her, under the guise of helping her steady herself. "Easy there," he said.

"Sorry about that," Paige said a bit breathlessly. "Mary's had me running back and forth all morning—I'm late to meet with James and shadow him."

Dan had to fight down an irrational stab of jealousy. Of course Paige would be shadowing different people around the ward until she had learned the ropes. Their schedules weren't even the same, so there was actually no way she could be shadowing Dan all the time. But he couldn't help but wish Mary had stuck her with Andrew or someone else who was a little less attractive.

"Do you know where you're going?" Dan asked. He had a bit of a break for the moment anyway, and playing the hero never hurt things.

"Not really," Paige confessed, just as he'd expected. "I mean, it's Ward Three, and I assume that's over near Ward Two, but..." She laughed a little. "This place is *huge* compared to where I used to work!"

"Let me show you," Dan offered. "Especially with elevators only sporadically placed around the building, it can get a little tricky."

"That would be great," Paige said gratefully. "But don't you have patients that you need to be seeing?"

"Not at the moment," Dan said. "And even if I did, I can spare five minutes to make sure that you get to Ward Three all right." Paige smiled at him. "How's your friend, anyway?" he asked as they walked.

Paige shrugged a little. "Oh, you know. Still acting like the world is ending and eating copious amounts of shitty takeout."

"Not unlike some of our patients, if you substitute shitty takeout for shitty hospital food," Dan observed.

Paige snorted. "Yeah, I guess so. She'll be fine, though."

"That's good," Dan said.

"I haven't forgotten about dinner either," Paige said boldly. "My work schedule is insane this week, though. I've got Monday off, or else it would have to be, like, tomorrow morning, because I'm working the night shift today."

"I have tomorrow off." He said it before he really thought it through. They obviously couldn't go for dinner if he took her out in the morning. And brunch was more of a friends thing. He needed to figure out how to make it into more of a relationship thing... "Why don't you come over to my place and I'll cook breakfast for you?" he asked. "I make some mean waffles." They could save the dinner date for another time. Hopefully she liked a man who cooked.

Paige certainly looked happy with that prospect. "That would be so great," she said. "Honestly, I usually get home after night shifts and don't really know what to do with myself. I mean, I know that I need food and usually I'm hungry, but I never really have the energy to cook, and most takeout places aren't open that early. But I also don't really want to be out in public anymore by that point!"

Dan laughed. "Yeah, I know the feeling." He stopped walking and jerked his chin towards the hallway that they were about to enter. "Anyway, this is Ward Three, and I think James is probably waiting in the lobby area right down the hall. But I'll see you tomorrow morning. I'll text you the address."

"Great," Paige said. This time, she was the one to lean up on her tiptoes and kiss Dan on the cheek. "You're such a darling. See you soon!"

Of course, the next morning, there was no cute little dress, but Paige was somehow beautiful in unassuming sweatpants and a teeshirt, with her hair pulled back in a messy bun. "Gosh, it smells amazing," she said as Dan let her in.

Dan laughed and pulled her in for a quick hug. "Thanks," he said. "I've been slaving away over a stove all morning."

"I thought you were just making waffles," Paige said.

Dan shrugged. "I threw together some bacon and sausage as well, and for the waffles, I've got some strawberries simmering on the stove too. And then there's coffee, juice, tea, water—whatever you want." Meanwhile, he led her into the joint kitchen and living room so she could see the proof for herself.

"You're a keeper," Paige said, shaking her head, a smile on her face. "Do you need help with anything?"

"Nah, it's fine," Dan said. "Why don't you have a seat—we can sit either at the table or on the sofa, whichever you'd prefer. The sofa's definitely more comfortable after a long shift, though, and I am definitely not judging you."

Paige grinned and sat carefully on the couch. Dan finished up cooking breakfast and started putting things on plates, still marveling that he was putting this much effort into sleeping with the woman. But he could only imagine that it would be worth it. Not only was she incredibly attractive, but he would bet that she hadn't had that many partners in the past. It would be flattering to make that list.

"What can I get you to drink?" he called over.

"Coffee would be great," Paige said. "And maybe some water too. I'm always dehydrated after a shift, no matter what I do."

"Coming right up," Dan said, setting the plates down in front of her. He brought their drinks and then sat next to her on the couch, purposefully sitting too close to her, so that their legs were pressed together. He was pleased when she didn't move away. "Dig in, and bon appetit," he said.

Paige didn't hesitate. "Oh wow," she said after her first bite of waffles. "Dan, these are amazing. Are you sure you're a doctor and not a cook?"

Dan laughed a little. "To be fair, waffles are pretty simple to whip up," he said. "Anyway, it was my mother's recipe originally. I've made a couple changes to it, but it's mostly still just the way she makes them."

"Aww," Paige cooed. "I'm sure your mother would be proud."

Dan snorted. To be honest, his mother wouldn't be happy about the way he was using her waffles to get this beautiful woman to fall into bed with him. But she didn't have to know about all of that.

Paige took another bite of her food. "I swear you missed your true calling in life," she said. "Not that I don't think you're a great doctor or anything like that; you're really good with the patients and..." She trailed off. "Gosh, I feel like I've really just put my foot in my mouth. Sorry. I just meant–"

Dan smiled a little, holding up a hand to halt her stammered apologies. "It's really fine," he said amusedly. "I'm glad you like the food. Your enthusiasm is flattering. Now stop babbling and eat!"

Paige laughed and grinned at him, taking another bite of her meal.

**Chapter Five**

When Dan finally got to take Paige to dinner, it was almost by accident. They happened to bump into one another outside the hospital. "Hey, how've you been?" Paige asked him.

"Fine," Dan said. "Just coming off shift, so I'm a bit exhausted and need to get some food in me. Was thinking of going over to Sue's."

Paige laughed. "Actually, same thing here. I'm just coming off shift and someone mentioned that Sue's is a good place to grab a good hot dinner. I normally would wait until I was back home, but I think I'd fall asleep on the bus if I didn't get some food in me first!"

Dan smiled at her. "Yeah, Sue's is a great place—really popular with a lot of us working here. Perfect comfort food at any hour of the day or night."

"Just what I need," Paige said. She paused. "I can't promise that I'll be much for conversation given how tired I am, but if you wanted to sit together..."

"I mean, it would be weird for us to walk in together and sit separately, wouldn't it?" Dan teased, starting to lead her towards the diner. Paige giggled. "I'm just lucky it's *you* that I ran into. I wouldn't be able to stand the company of just *anyone* after the shift that I had..."

Paige slipped her arm into his and leaned into him a little as they walked, and Dan inwardly cheered at his apparent success. It wouldn't be long now before he could take her to bed with him, and then it would be time to move on to the next woman.

Something in that idea made him pause, though. It would be a shame to cut Paige out of his life again. They had great conversations, both in person and through text during their busy weeks. He could still picture her sat there on his couch looking rumpled after a long shift, eating the breakfast that he had made for her. And there was something about that sweet domesticity that he *wanted*, in a way he never had before.

"Penny for your thoughts?" Paige asked him.

Dan blinked down at her and then turned her so that they were facing one another. His hand lightly cupped her cheek, his finger stroking along her sharp cheekbone as he leaned down to kiss her. He didn't deepen the kiss the way he normally would; instead, he kept it chaste and light, soft and inquisitive. When he pulled away, Paige's eyes had fluttered shut.

She blinked them open to look at him. "Wasn't really expecting that," she said quietly. She shook her head. "Dan, we work together. And I like your company. I'm not sure that this is the best idea."

Dan frowned, wondering if he had pushed things too soon. But he'd known the woman for *weeks* already, and it was about time he made some sort of a move on her. Their pace was practically glacial compared to how Dan normally went about things with women.

Paige took a deep breath and then leaned up on her toes to return the kiss. It was just as close-mouthed as before, but she used a hint more pressure as she slid her warm lips across his. Then, she pulled away, looking decidedly bashful.

"I thought this was a bad idea," Dan said, smirking at her.

Paige grinned shyly at him and ducked her head. "Yeah, well. I can't say that I don't want it."

Dan grinned as well and slung his arm around her shoulders. "Come on, let me buy you dinner finally," he said, leading her into the diner.

Dan glanced around the diner as they followed the waitress to one of the booths in the back. Fortunately, there didn't seem to be many of their colleagues there in the diner, and the colleagues who were there weren't ones that would think anything of the two of them eating dinner together. If, say, Craig had been there, he might have mentioned something about Dan's player attitude to Paige—his exploits were more or less known by many of the other men on the ward. But the coast seemed to be clear.

"So what's good here?" Paige asked.

Dan shrugged, looking over the menu. "They do a really solid breakfast, and that's an all-day thing. Personally, I'm more in a dinner kind of mood, so I'll probably go for the chicken fried steak. Their burgers are pretty good too. And...well, honestly, I've never had a bad dish here."

Paige laughed. "So I've got options, I guess," she said. "A burger sounds good, though, so I guess that at least narrows it down." She looked over the menu for a moment longer and then snapped it shut, waiting patiently for the waitress to come over to take their order.

"So I feel like you've asked me all about myself but I haven't asked about you yet," Paige said to Dan once the waitress had bounced off to put their order in with the kitchen. "What do *you* do outside of work?"

Dan smiled. "Well, cooking is one thing. I do quite a bit of that. For me, it's relaxing. I can put on a little music, really get into the rhythm of it. And I watch bad TV too. I go hiking a lot on my days off, or just have a little wander around the city. I have a hard time not being active on those days, when I have to have such a high level of energy on my work days."

"That makes sense," Paige said. "And what about your family? You said you grew up here, so I assume they still live close?"

"Yeah, my mother lives a little outside the city now but I go out to visit her pretty regularly or she'll come into the city and meet me for lunch sometimes. My dad actually moved back to his home in the

Northeast, so I don't see him much, but usually he'll make it out here or I'll make it out there a few times a year."

"Brothers and sisters?" Paige asked.

Dan grinned. "Only child."

They continued like that for a while, and Dan realized with a weird jolt that he was telling Paige more about himself than he had really told anyone in years. There was just something about her, something so open and honest, that he couldn't seem to stop himself from telling her everything.

When their food finally came, Dan broke off what he was saying—a somewhat embarrassing anecdote about one of the worst term papers he'd submitted when he was in grad school—and blinked at Paige for a moment. She was leaning forward on the table, her head propped in her hand. She somehow managed to look tired and entirely content at the same time.

"Sorry, I've been babbling at you," he said. "You must be sick of hearing me."

Paige laughed a little and straightened up so the waitress could put her food in front of her. "I've been enjoying it," she said. "Like I said earlier, I'm really exhausted at the moment, so I'm not sure I could really keep up a good conversation with you. It's good hearing you talk about yourself."

"I don't usually," Dan confessed before he could stop himself.

Paige raised an eyebrow at him. "You don't usually what?" she asked.

Dan shrugged a little awkwardly. "I don't usually talk about myself like this."

Paige looked surprised and then a bit pleased. "Guess maybe you might like me a little?" she asked teasingly.

Dan frowned and then shook his head. "Paige, there's something you have to know about me," he said. "I'm...not the best guy. I mean, if you asked Craig or any of the other guys that we work with—"

"I know," Paige interrupted. She fixed Dan with a challenging stare. "I've already been warned to steer clear of you, ever since that first day when I shadowed you. Everyone says you're really charming but it's just so that you can sleep with every female who goes through there. But I don't think that's really the case, is it?"

Dan shrugged. "I mean, that was my goal—charm you until you were willing to go to bed with me. You're incredibly attractive, you know. And then I would probably have never contacted you again."

Paige frowned as well. "But you're telling me all of this now because...?" she asked. "You reveal what an asshole you are and then say that I make you want to be a better person, and *then* I decide to have sex with you and you never call again?"

"No," Dan said, shaking his head. He picked at the edge of his napkin. "The thing about it is, I actually really have enjoyed your company, and... Well, like I said, I never really open up to people like this. Maybe it's time I did."

"You're going to have to be more specific than that," Paige said. "You kissed me before. Are we or aren't we...?"

Dan took a deep breath, staring over at the woman across from him. He knew relationships were difficult, but he also felt like the pleasure of a long-term relationship with Paige would be even more incredible and inspiring than a stupid one-night fling.

"No sex until the timing is right," he told Paige. "Until we *both* feel the timing is right and that we're not just...rushing into this, I guess."

Paige smiled a little at him. "Okay," she said. She reached out and clasped Dan's hand in hers.

# SARAH'S PRAYER

## BOBBI JOE YATES

## Chapter One

Pastor Michael seemed more agitated this session, Sarah noticed, making sure to write that down in her notepad. Not that that was something she would ever use against him, but it was useful information in gaining insight into his psyche. He'd been coming to her for marriage counseling for three months now, and she still didn't really know what the deeper issue interrupting his marriage was.

"There are sometimes when I just have to see you without Eileen," Michael said suddenly, spinning to face her and pinning her with what Sarah called his Church Gaze: stern eyes that could pierce her soul if they chose to. "I know you know her, probably better than I do, since you both seem to understand one another and I don't know if I've ever understood her. But Sarah, you don't know what it's like, living with her, doing everything with her."

Sarah nodded sagely. "You feel you've grown together too much," she said.

Michael laughed bitterly. "Quite the opposite," he said.

Sarah frowned. "You feel that she is growing away from the church and leaving you behind?" she asked.

Michael shook his head. "No, it's nothing like that," he said, sounding tormented. "Instead, I know I should be devoting my life towards God and towards the church. But instead, I-" He broke off, looking guilty.

"You...?" Sarah prodded questioningly. Michael was one of her more frustrating clients since he had a tendency to frequently break off in the middle of a thought. She was starting to realize he would break off whenever he felt something he was about to say might be blasphemous, but she was also starting to realize that those supposedly blasphemous things that he was about to say were the key to solving this whole thing. It kept her on the edge of her seat each time, waiting for the one time when he managed to finish a thought without the fear of God stopping him.

Michael stared at her for a long moment, and Sarah thought with a sinking heart that he wasn't going to finish the thought. But then, he wet his lips and cleared his throat a little. "I find that I'm...drawn to someone else," he admitted.

Sarah blinked at him, surprised to get that truth from him. Of course, it didn't mean there was nothing wrong with his marriage since there had to be something driving this principled, moral man towards another woman, but if the main reason he and Eileen were coming to marriage counseling was because Michael fancied himself in love with another woman, it certainly changed things. She doubted he would ever act on those feelings, for one thing, and for another, that meant this was probably just a bit of a midlife crisis on his part—it wasn't that he was dissatisfied with his current situation, he just thought he should make a bit of a change. She just had to make him see that he could do that from inside of the relationship.

"Eileen knows you're drawn to someone else?" Sarah asked slowly.

Michael sighed and slumped down on one of the sofas, his long legs akimbo. "I don't know," he answered honestly. "This other woman, she's not the reason we first started coming here. But she's becoming...more of the reason we're still coming here."

"Has Eileen seen you interact with this other woman?"

Michael exhaled noisily. "Yes, she has. The woman is a member of our parish, and we talk often—even outside of church functions. I do my best not to let things escalate beyond talking—absolutely no touching or anything like that. As much as I long to..."

Sarah frowned at him. "Well, that's good. That shows a reluctance to give up on what you have with Eileen." She paused, trying to think of a delicate way to phrase what she wanted to say next. "And what does, uh, God have to say about...all of this?" Well, so much for delicacy.

Michael dropped his head into his hands. "I'm too close to the matter," he told her, his voice raw with emotion. "I'm afraid I'm not able to objectively interpret the will of God on this matter."

Sarah stared at him for a moment, shock written on her face. That had to be tormenting him, after all his years of service to the church and to God. She was struck with the sudden desire to move to the couch next to him and lay a hand on his shoulder.

When she did so, Michael blinked over at her, looking momentarily not like the stern pastor she'd come to know but rather like a lost, lonely, rather ordinary man. Up close like this, she could see the bags beneath his eyes, hinting at fitful nights of sleep.

She lightly squeezed his shoulder.

Michael brought his hand slowly up to cover hers, but then he yanked away as though he'd been burnt, standing abruptly and looking at his watch. "I'm afraid I have to go," he said, nearly tripping over himself in his haste.

"Michael," Sarah said, surprised at how firm her voice was. Michael paused at the door and half-turned back towards her. "Running away from your feelings isn't going to get you anywhere," she scolded.

The pastor seemed to deflate a little. "I don't want to do something I'll regret," he said hoarsely. "I think that Eileen and I need to stop seeing you. It's been a pleasure—believe me, it has—but I can't..."

Sarah frowned and took a couple steps towards him, holding out her hand imploringly. "Wait a minute, Michael," she said quietly. "Come on, let's sit down on the couch and talk for a minute. Explain to me what the problem is."

Michael looked like he was about ready to tear his hair out. "It's you, don't you get it?" the man said, sounding pained. "Ever since Eileen and I started coming here, I've become more and more...smitten by you." He blushed and looked away from her.

Sarah stared at him for a long moment, totally lost for words. After all these months of trying to get truth out of him, she wanted, on one hand, to rejoice at how open he was finally being with her. But on the other hand, she couldn't deny the awkward position that he was putting her in. There had to be something in her contract against her taking advantage of people who came to her for counseling. And even if there wasn't, there had to be something morally wrong with it.

But she was fixated with the way that for the first time, she could see what a handsome man the pastor was. His dark hair fell in waves that didn't quite reach his eyes, which stood out from his chiseled cheekbones as though the Greeks had sculpted him from a block of pristine marble. When he blinked those clear blue eyes...

She swallowed hard.

"I know," Michael sighed, looking away from her. "You haven't even finalized your divorce yet. And I haven't even asked for a divorce from Eileen yet, even though I know in my heart of hearts that this clearly isn't working. I don't know where it went wrong, even. She's been the perfect wife for me, and yet I... It started so small. We thought we could fix it. But the more we try to fix it, the more I become convinced that it's not something we could fix. And it's not just that I'm finding myself more attracted to you than I ever was to her. It's just..." He trailed off, shaking his head. "I try to tell myself that it's a test from God, but that no longer comforts me like it used to."

Sarah tried desperately to process his words, to formulate some sort of response. She thought for a minute about David, about everything that she'd had in the life that she'd built with him. About the day that David had told her that he wanted a divorce. The trouble was, everything that she felt for David ground to a halt when she thought of those divorce papers, the copy of which she kept buried in her sock drawer, a quiet reminder of her failure.

"I don't make a good wife," she blurted suddenly, surprised to feel the tears in her eyes.

For a moment, Michael looked torn, as though he wanted desperately to come to her side, to comfort her. But there was something there that was holding him back, just as she might expect. He stumbled a couple steps back, reaching his hand out to grasp the doorknob. "Sarah," he said, voice sounding absolutely wrecked with his feelings. "Sarah, I have to go." And without another word, he fled from her office.

Sarah sank down on one of the plush couches and curled into herself, trying her best not to sob.


**Chapter Two**

The rest of the day passed in a bit of a blur for Sarah. She had a couple other appointments, but fortunately, there was nothing too tricky that she had to deal with: she didn't know that she would have been able to figure out the intricacies that plagued some of her clients. Indeed, she could hardly figure out the questions that she meant to ask her less-tricky clients.

"Sarah, are you feeling okay?" Carrie asked her in her final session of the day.

Sarah blinked over at the woman, trying desperately to remember what the woman's husband had just been speaking about. But she couldn't seem to remember. She shook her head slowly. "I'm afraid I need to end this session early," she said quietly. "I'm sorry, I just– I'm not feeling so good tonight."

Carrie smiled gently at her, while George looked like he wanted to roll his eyes but didn't dare to. They both politely got up to leave, making her promise that she would go home and sleep with her unexpected free time.

Instead, Sarah lay back on one of the couches and closed her eyes, unable to face the whitewashed ceiling and sterile-but-cozy environment that she and David had designed in that office.

She lay there for a long time, but she was no closer to mental resolution by the time she finally sat up. She had to go home. She would need to pick up dinner on the way home, because there was nothing left in the house that she could make into any sort of respectable dinner. And then she would need to sort through her notes from the day and get everything in order for the next day. Maybe she would watch something stupid on television for the end of the night. Then she would set her alarm and fall into her lonely, cold bed. The next morning, she would wake up early and start it all over again.

That's what her life had become, After David: a series of tasks that she knew she needed to complete. And she didn't want to say that she felt any sort of pride with each new day that she managed to tick her way through, but...well, it was kind of true that she did. And, hey, whatever got you out of bed in the morning, right?

When she got home to a house where all the lights were on, her first instinct was to blink her eyes and look around, as though ten years after moving to this house, she might have accidentally parked in one of her neighbor's driveways. But no, this was definitely 116 Fulker's Drive—she could see the house number clearly in the beam of her headlights.

For a moment, she thought she might have left the house lights all on that morning. But while she might have turned on the kitchen light in the early light of the day, there was no way she would have ever needed the light in the living room. There had to be someone else in there.

She sat staring at the house for a long time, her fingers white on the leather steering wheel. It was possible that someone had broken in. But what would they have taken from her, anyways? She didn't have much, since they'd started the process of the divorce. David had always bought most of their things, and she hadn't felt much like fighting him when he'd claimed it all back in the divorce. Her lawyer had tried to argue, back when this had first started, but when Sarah had refused to go along with it, her lawyer had got sick of it and just let her dictate their course of action. There were very few things that held meaning to her there in the house, and they weren't the sorts of things that would attract the eye of a thief.

She didn't call the police. Instead, after a long moment, she switched off her headlights and stepped out of the car, heading slowly into the house.

When she saw David sitting there on the couch, her first thought was that she must be more tired than she'd thought she was. She rubbed tiredly at her eyes, but when she opened them again, he was still there staring back at her. And when he moved, well. That was when she really started to believe that he was truly there. No matter how she'd memorized his movements over the years, she was sure a figment of her imagination wouldn't achieve the level of grace that he did.

"What are you doing here?" she asked hoarsely.

David paused, looking at her. "You look like hell," he told her, but his words were gentle, as though it were five years ago and he wanted to pull her into his arms and help her relax after a long day.

Sarah fought back a wave of tears. "I can't deal with you here tonight," she told him. "I can't..." She was in tears before she really realized it, all the stress of the meeting with Michael catching up to her. She didn't know what she wanted with her future, but it seemed like the universe itself was pressuring her to decide. And how was she to make that choice?

"Oh Sarah," David breathed, breaching the distance between the two of them and pulling the woman into his arms. "Oh Sarah."

They were both silent for a long time, both swaying slightly to the sound of some unheard song.

It was Sarah who finally pulled away. "I can't–" she started.

"Shh," David said, even going so far as to place a finger over her lips. He squeezed his eyes shut briefly, the most emotion Sarah had seen out of him in months—if not years. "Sarah, I don't want to go through on the divorce," he said.

Sarah stared at him and then, despite herself, started to laugh. "David, we've been processing this divorce for *months* now," she reminded him. She waved her hand around the half-barren house.

"You've taken all your things from here. You've moved into the house on Somerset Street. And–"

Again, David placed the finger over her lips. "Sarah," he said, his voice sounding hurt, "just listen to me for a minute, would you? Please."

Sarah shook her head, though. "Oh no," she said, drawing back away. "Oh no. No, you don't get to ask that, not now. Not when you wouldn't tell me why you were divorcing me until you had served me the papers. Not when–"

David shook his head. "I've done a lot of thinking, Sarah," he said, sounding hurt. "Sarah, you don't know how it's felt like, divorcing you. When all I really wanted was to talk things over with you. But it wasn't like we could go to a marriage counselor. You would have picked them apart, point by point. Everything would have been on your terms. I didn't know how to... I just didn't know what I was doing. I'm sorry."

Sarah shook her head again. "We can't do this," she whispered.

For the first time, it was David pulling away. "Is there someone else?" he asked.

Sarah was silent for a long time. They stared at one another. Sarah could remember falling in love with David. He had been so handsome—*was* so handsome, although in an entirely different sense from Michael. Where Michael had that classical, chiseled handsomeness, David's looks could only be described as *pretty*—but it was a prettiness that transcended genders. It was there in his smooth, thin fingers—in the graceful way that he moved—in the angular features of his face.

And there had been the care that he'd shown for her. And his sense of humor. It was his personality, above everything, that she'd fallen for.

But she could remember the day he'd asked for a divorce, clearer than any other day in her life. She could have told you what both of them were wearing, where they were, what the very *air* around them smelled like. She could have told you the song that was playing out the doors of the nearby shop.

She couldn't have told you how it felt, having her heart broken like that. That was the one thing that she knew she would never have the words for.

"There might be someone else," she finally admitted, unable to meet his eyes. She swallowed hard.

David exhaled noisily through his nose. "I thought there might be," he finally said. He laughed a little. "I guess I had my epiphany moment too late, hmm?"

Sarah didn't know how to answer that. "I didn't say that there *was* someone," she finally pointed out, because by now, it was a conditioned response to be truthful to him. "I admitted that there *might* be someone." She ducked her head, wishing almost that she hadn't told him that. That was as good as challenging him to win her back, something that she didn't want.

David had been the one to ask her out. He'd been the one to ask her to move in with him. He'd been the one to ask her to meet his family. And he'd been the one to ask her to marry him. Everything about their relationship had been initiated by him; for once, she kind of wanted to make her own decisions.

What if she wanted to try this thing with Michael?

The thought came unbidden, and it caused her to blush a little. She picked at the edge of her sleeve as though it were the most fascinating thing in the world. "David, I'm going to need you to leave now," she said in a voice that she hardly recognized as hers.

"I want to take you out," he said quietly. He didn't move from his spot, and he held up his hands placatingly.

Sarah stared at him. But she couldn't forget all the memories they had made together. "When?" she finally asked, her voice hardly audible.

## Chapter Three

The one thing she could be happy for, she reflected, was that David wasn't stupid enough to bring her back to the place that they'd had their first date. As much as she loved that place, there were too many memories attached to it, and she knew it would hurt to be back there, with their relationship in its current state. Instead, he had selected a Moroccan restaurant that they had never eaten at before. Sarah appreciated the choice, especially because she knew he didn't like Moroccan food that much. He was making this about her.

They were both clearly nervous, she reflected, as he rushed around to open her door for her.

She blushed and looked up at him through her lashes as she arranged her shawl around her. "David, you don't need to impress me," she said quietly. "Remember, you already got me to marry you once." It wasn't meant as a dig; instead, it was more a statement of fact. But she could see the way he winced.

"Sarah, I want you to forget about that tonight," he said quietly. "I want you to focus on now, on tonight. I want to–"

Sarah burst out laughing, unable to help herself. Not only was that unhealthy, but– "That's impossible," she told him. "Although if what you're trying to tell me is that you can forget the fact that we were once married, well. I guess I can see why–"

"That's not it," David interrupted. He scrubbed a hand over his face, looking momentarily exhausted. "Sarah, that's not it at all. You know that. You know I could never forget what it was like to be married to you." He smiled a little at her. "We were such good friends, weren't we?"

Sarah sighed and looked away. "David," she said warningly.

"Okay," David said, catching her arm and tugging her towards the doorway of the restaurant. "Let's forget about that—about all of that. For tonight, for just one night, I want to start anew. If we can. I think we can." He paused, eyes hesitantly searching her face. "I want to act like this is our first date, like we're going into this with no baggage behind us," he told her. "Of course we were married. Of course we know one another better than most people do, first date or fiftieth date. But I want to pretend like–"

"I don't know if I can do that," Sarah said, before he could go any further. She shook her head. "Even being here, with all of our baggage—that's enough for me to sort through."

David was silent for a moment. He lightly brushed a lock of hair behind Sarah's ear. "I always loved how blunt you were," he said.

Sarah sighed and pushed him away a little. "We can love however many small parts of the other person's personality," she said. "But in the long run, that doesn't mean we're going to be okay, married to one another."

David nodded sagely. "But Sarah, what else are you going to look for?" he asked.

Sarah frowned, thinking about Michael even though she knew she should be focusing her thought on this current date. Somehow, though, she knew that Michael would have understood this better than anyone else—the idea of being married to someone, loving someone so much, and then having to come to the realization that maybe you were never meant to be together.

She would have expected Michael to have that same understanding as her, but then again, she had expected Michael to remain happily married to her for the rest of their lives.

She followed him into the restaurant.

They were mostly silent while they looked over the menu and placed their orders. When the waitress had walked away, Sarah laughed a little nervously, folding her hands on the table. "I don't really know what to say," she admitted. "This has all just kind of been...out of the blue."

David sighed and reached over, taking her hands in his. "I've really missed you lately," he said quietly. "I've missed *us*. And I've been trying to work on...well, everything. Myself. I'd like for you to see me as I am now. I'm happier."

Sarah shook her head and pulled her hands away. "You can't just..." She shook her head again.

"Sarah, we needed to take a break, you know that as well as I do," David insisted. "We were stagnating. We were doing the same things over and over and over again, and having the same fights over and over and over again. There's only so much of that that a relationship can take. We needed to find ourselves again as separate entities so that we could—"

"I don't," Sarah interrupted.

"You don't what?" David asked, faltering a little.

"I don't know that we needed a break," Sarah said. Her hands spasmed, momentarily clenching into fists. "That's the thing. This whole divorce thing...that was your idea. I didn't even realize there was a problem, I didn't even realize we were...stagnating, if that's what you think we were doing. You didn't even give me a chance to fix things, a chance to work through things. You just told me it was over and that there was nothing else I could do."

They were both silent for a moment.

"It was hard for me as well," David said quietly. "Don't forget that. Don't think I didn't think it through, torment myself with the thought of it day after day for months."

"Is that supposed to make me feel better about it?" Sarah snapped. "The fact remains—I trusted you. You were my best friend, you were my everything. And then suddenly you were just...gone. Without even a concrete reason. Do you know how long it took me to put myself back together?"

"But that's it, Sarah, that's exactly what we needed," David pleaded. "That's exactly what I'm saying. We've both worked on ourselves, found ourselves as individual entities again, and—"

Sarah stood abruptly. "I don't know what I expected from tonight, but I don't think I can do this. It's too painful, David." She took a deep breath. "I still want that divorce, even if you don't."

David caught her wrist with one hand, pinching the bridge of his nose with the other hand. "Wait, Sarah. Can you just sit down, please? Can we talk about this? I want to know what you've been up to lately, what–"

Sarah pulled her arm away. "I wanted to talk," she said hoarsely. "I wanted to talk, back when you wanted to get a divorce. And you wouldn't let me. I don't want to talk anymore. I want to put you in the past and move on with my life. It's taken me ages to get to this point, and I don't want to undo all the work that I've done. So I'm going to leave."

"You don't want to get hurt again," David said. "That's what it really comes down to, isn't it?"

Sarah paused for a moment, searching inside herself for the answer to that question. "It's not that I don't want to get hurt again," she said, glancing back at the man. "I'm sure I'll open up to someone else, when the time is right and I'm ready for it. But I don't want to get hurt by *you* again—no."

With that, she turned and strode out of the restaurant.


**Chapter Four**

That night, Sarah lay there in bed thinking about her two options. On the one hand, of course, there was David. She'd married the man for a reason. He was beautiful, he was kind, and she'd always pictured a future with him. She'd thought that one day, they would have children, that they would...

But she couldn't ignore the ways that they'd grown apart from one another. And she couldn't forget that hopeless feeling that she'd had when he'd asked her for a divorce, totally blindsiding her with his conviction that they were never meant for one another, despite the harmonious life they'd built with one another.

On the other hand, there was Michael. Michael was a good man, and he seemed to understand her better than she could ever have expected. He was charismatic and witty, and he always kept up a good conversation. He was having trouble in his own marriage, so he would understand where she was coming from. And for whatever reason, he had said that he liked her.

Without conscious direction from her mind, she found her right hand grasped around the phone, her left fingers punching out Michael's phone number, which she hadn't even realized she had memorized.

No one picked up, which wasn't too surprising since it was—she squinted at the clock—three in the morning. She blushed and dropped the phone back onto her nightstand. Anyway, it was probably for the best: what the hell did she think she was going to say to him?

The thing was, though, she wanted to tell him about David coming back, about him asking her to not go through with the divorce after all. She wanted to talk to Michael, to sort through all her complicated feelings about this situation. To tell him that in the end, Michael himself was one of the major obstacles keeping her from happily going back to David and the life she had previously led.

Maybe they had been stagnating. The thought of returning to the same life that she'd been living for the better part of twenty years made her frown. She didn't think things would be easy with Michael—he would need to go through with a divorce, and who knew what the parish would think about that. And she did like Eileen; she didn't want to hurt the woman. And then there were all of the challenges of a new relationship: getting to know the other person, learning to compromise with them, getting used to their unique quirks... There was a possibility that she would choose Michael over David, only to have both of those relationships fall through.

But then she would find someone else. Sarah was actually surprised at how firmly her mind supplied that thought. When David had first left her, she'd thought she would be alone forever.

She smiled a little, the marriage counselor part of herself recognizing what a big step this was for her. Finally, it seemed like her mind calmed a little, and she drifted off to sleep.

In the morning, it was back to chaos in her mind, but she managed to push through it to do her work as usual. At least until Michael appeared in her doorway, twisting his hands together.

"Are you busy?" the man asked.

Sarah barely spared a glance for the pile of paperwork that she was sorting through. "What's wrong?" she asked.

Michael took a couple hesitant steps into the room. "I wanted to let you know that..." He trailed off, looking uncertain. Then, he took a deep breath. "I wanted to let you know that I filed for a divorce from Eileen," he told her. He took another couple steps and sat rigidly on the edge of one of the couches. "She's a very good woman, but I don't know...how to do right by her anymore. She deserves better than me."

"That's a dangerous way to think," Sarah said clinically, looking down at the pen she had been using. "You need to accept your flaws, and you need to allow the other person to accept them as well. If Eileen is willing to–"

"Stop," Michael interrupted. When Sarah looked up at him, surprise on her face, he shook his head, a small smile on his lips. "This isn't a session," he told her. "This is two...friends...having a conversation. I don't need you to psychoanalyze everything. In fact, I'd prefer that you didn't."

Sarah blinked at him. "Friends?" she asked.

Michael looked momentarily uncertain. "Well, I hoped so, anyway. I mean, I won't be your client anymore since you kind of have to have a marriage in order to need marriage counseling, but maybe I could take you out for coffee sometime."

Sarah stared at him for a long moment and then smiled hesitantly. "I'd like that," she said quietly. She picked up her pen, twirling it between her fingers. "We should wait until after your divorce is finalized," she said, carefully not looking at the man. "You have...a lot of influence around town. You wouldn't want them to think..."

"You're right," Michael said, standing abruptly. "You're very right." He smiled at her and gave an aborted wave. Sarah couldn't help but smile at the way the stern, aloof pastor had suddenly been stripped away and replaced by this nervous, entirely-human man. "I'll see you in a few months, then, Sarah. Take care of yourself."


**Chapter Five**

Sarah tugged nervously at her sleeves while she waiting for Michael to reach her. It seemed like every member of the congregation wanted to thank him for that morning's sermon—which admittedly had been one of the most moving ones that Sarah had ever heard, but still. She felt like she was practically vibrating out of her skin, waiting anxiously for him.

The last person in the line of people waiting to speak to the man was Eileen, Sarah was surprised to see. Of course, she'd seen the woman there in the church, but she hadn't expected her to approach Michael. It had taken Sarah much longer before she'd worked up the courage to put aside her feelings of hurt and speak to David again.

Eileen took Michael's hands in hers, leaning in close and murmuring something. Whatever it was that she had said, Michael laughed at it, and Sarah had to quash an irrational flare of jealousy and uncertainty. They both had pasts; that was something that was unavoidable. She couldn't feel jealous every time Michael and Eileen interacted with one another, especially not when they were still living in the same small town and still going to the same church. She wouldn't have wanted Michael to feel jealous about her history with David either. It was something that was in the past, and it would stay there.

Besides, Michael had chosen to end his marriage with the woman. Sarah knew she had to trust in that.

Eileen finally broke away from Michael and smiled knowingly over her shoulder at Sarah. Sarah blinked at her and turned questioning eyes to Michael, who gave a little shrug as he made his way over to her. It made sense that he had told her, she supposed, when she really thought about it. In a town like theirs, she was likely to find out anyway. Better that she hear about it from Michael instead of someone else.

Michael finally reached her and held out his arm to her. "Shall we?" he asked in his deep voice.

Sarah smiled hesitantly up at him. "Let's," she agreed, slipping her hand into the inside of the man's elbow. "That really was a great sermon, you know," she said as they walked out of the churchyard. "Everything about forgiveness and... Well, a lot of it really hit home to me."

"I should hope so," Michael said, the corners of his lips quirking upwards. "I wrote most of that sermon while Eileen and I were coming to you for marriage counseling. A lot of the themes were the themes that we covered during our sessions. And I finished the sermon last week, after the divorce was finalized. I'm sure you, as a divorcee yourself, understood that sermon better than almost everyone else in town."

Sarah was silent for a long moment. "Do you regret it?" she asked.

Michael paused and drew Sarah around to face him. "Not one bit," he said seriously, his piercing gaze glued firmly on her. "Sarah, Eileen and I had something very special—as, I imagine, you and David did. But..." He reached out and tucked a lock of hair gently behind Sarah's ear. "You don't know how much I want to kiss you right now," he said in an undertone. "But I don't think that would be appropriate, given how recent my divorce was."

Sarah burst out laughing. "You sound like a teenager," she said. "Can't keep your hands off me?"

Michael smiled at her. "Well, you are gorgeous, I hope you realize." He shook his head and turned them so that they were walking again. "But for now, let's get to know one another better. Tell me about yourself, Ms. Sarah Walker."

Sarah shook her head, bumping her shoulder against his. "That's a pretty broad question," she said. "I'm not sure where to begin."

"Let's start with yesterday," Michael said, laughing a little. "What did you do yesterday? But before you answer, just know that I've set myself a goal: one day, I want to know everything about you. So you'd better be ready to tell me *all* about yourself. It just doesn't have to all be now."

Sarah laughed as well. "Okay," she said. "Sounds like a plan."

She smiled shyly at the man as he held the door open for her and ushered her into the coffee shop. For the first time since her divorce, she could feel hope blooming in her chest.

# TIME ON FIRE

## JENNIFER COLE

It was cold on the day of the funeral. Guests arrived covered in snow and ice. Laura stood at the front of the funeral parlor all day thanking people for coming to pay their condolences to her late husband, Tom. It was a closed casket. His death was far too gruesome for Laura to allow people to see. He was around fire almost every day, and it wasn't surprising that he burned to death after getting caught at the scene of a fire. He was always too brave for his own good. It's what made him a great firefighter, but it didn't always make him the best husband.

In fact, Laura and Tom were having problems before he died. He was not great at opening up, and it made communication a huge issue in their relationship. It was the main problem in their short four-year marriage. Laura just wanted to know what he was thinking and how he was feeling, but she felt so shut out. She told him over and over again that she needed to hear him say how he felt about her and their life together, but he just couldn't seem to express himself. Just hours before she learned of the horrible accident, Laura was on the phone with a divorce lawyer discussing the process.

Everyone held Laura and gave her sad looks. She felt guilty, and she felt like she didn't deserve the sympathy. If only these people knew what was really going on! If only they had seen him that one night they might look sympathetic for another reason.

Laura and Tom grew up together. They went to the same middle school and the same high school. They were in different circles in school, though. Tom was a part of the cool group. He dates gorgeous girls, and he was in three different sports throughout the year. Laura, on the other hand, was a bit more reserved. She was going through an awkward phase that never seemed to hit Tom. She had zits, and she thought that she was fat. She always had a crush on Tom, but she never had the courage to dare talk to him. They would smile politely at each other in the hall since they had known each other for so long, but that was it. Laura got much more confident after college. She lost weight, she felt accomplished, and she didn't have those darn pimples anymore.

When she came home and saw Tom in his firefighter uniform, she wasn't afraid to go say hi. Two weeks later they were an official couple and about two years after that, they were married.

Looking back, Laura honestly couldn't remember why they got along so well. The physical attraction was definitely there, but she couldn't think of anything else.

"I'm so terribly sorry for your loss," a voice said.

"Huh? Oh, yeah. It's been quite a couple of days," Laura responded automatically.

"He was just so young."

"He was a very brave man. Thank you for coming."

"Well, honey, you know he's up there waiting for you."

"I like to think so. Yes."

The one thing that they don't tell you when you lose a family member is how darn repetitive it is. Laura couldn't actually say what she felt. She couldn't say that she was exhausted from making the arrangements, she couldn't say that she was bored of the funeral all ready, and she couldn't say that she was a tiny bit happy that it ended this way instead of divorce. She kept her grieving smile on, and she went through the proceedings like the mourning wife she was.

A young man who arrived by himself walked up to Laura and gave her a hug.

"It's such a travesty what happened," the man said. Laura was surprised by his affection. He seemed so touched by Tom's death. To be honest, it was the first time that Laura felt sad throughout the day. She wanted to hug him and comfort him.

"It was quite unexpected," Laura said.

"My name is Gary. I'd really like to get together sometime," the man said. "We both worked at the fire station. He was always the prankster, as you know. However, he had a big heart, too. I have a couple things that I"d like to share with you."

"That would be nice," Laura said. She never meant it.

When the day was finally over and she was able to go back home, the house felt different. It had a ghost in it. This used to be Laura and Tom's home. Laura and Tom's home didn't exist anymore, though, because Laura and Tom didn't exist. Their little suburban starter home was not filled with the hope and future plans that it once had. Laura tried to lay in the large king-sized bed, and she couldn't sleep. The next day, she put a For Sale sign in the front yard.

"And where are you planning to go?" Laura's mother asked when Laura told her the news.

"I don't know, ma. I'll go somewhere that I've never been. See things that I've never seen. Be someone that I am not."

"You can't run away from your problems, Laura."

"I'm not running away from my problems. I have nothing here for me. My job is a dead-end, and I don't have family or many friends. We moved here because this is the station that they assigned Tom. Now, I can go wherever I want. I have nothing holding me back."

"You make it sound like Tom was holding you back."

"You know that's not what I meant, ma."

"Well, you now you're always welcome back home if you need some time to figure things out. Your father is on the golf course almost every day, and I have my gardening. We won't be in your hair too much."

"I don't want to impose. Besides, I"ll be there in two weeks for Aunt Lilly's birthday."

"Well, take care of yourself, dear. I love you."

"I love you too, mom."

Laura sat down in her living room by herself with a glass of wine and a blanket over her. Her dog, Daisy, laid down at her feet sleeping. At least Daisy was there to help her feel less alone. It was a feeling that she was slowly getting used to. It was a feeling that was both terrifying and liberating at the same time. In a quick blur of just a couple of weeks, the house sold much more quickly than Laura anticipated, and the new family paid extra to move in as quickly as possible. Before she knew it, she had movers putting everything into storage temporarily, and she was off to who knows where.

*****

Laura sat in her car with Daisy in the passenger seat and a backseat full of suitcases. She tapped the steering wheel and looked around her with absolutely no idea of where to go. She was just blocks from her house, ready to leave her old life behind, but she didn't really plan for her new life that well. Eventually, Laura took a breath and started driving. She always liked Florida. She also liked Texas. There was Louisiana. Maybe she would go to Washington. Or Vermont. She liked skiing. Everything was so uncertain, but she just drove hoping to find an answer soon enough.

Laura drove for two days. She wasn't heading anywhere in particular, and she backtracked a bit. She spent nights in hotels and took breaks a couple of times a day to take long walks with Daisy.

Finally, she found a spot. She didn't even know what state she was in at first. She knew that she had been heading south for a very long time, and she was noticing the smell of barbecue and grass in the air. Everything was green, and there were more stars in the sky than she had ever seen. She was in a small town with a lot of small houses and shops. Everything looked old, and the roads were quiet. She drove around slowly looking for a motel or at least a diner. She could start looking for a house soon enough. Right now, she just wanted to get some sleep and some food and decide if this is where she wanted to build up a new life.

Laura found the Kentucky Suites on one of the main roads in town. It looked nice enough for her at the moment. She checked in. The room wasn't anything special, but it had a large, comfortable bed, a television, mini-fridge, ironing board, and it was clean. Plus, the facilities had laundry, an exercise room, a pool, and a hot tub. Laura decided that she was sick of driving aimlessly, and Laura paid for the room for a week in advance. She put away all of her clothes and sat in her room unsure of exactly what to do now. She knew that she should go explore the town and maybe start looking for a job, but she couldn't get herself to leave the hotel room. She ordered Chinese food and stayed inside thinking of Tom.

She hated Tom, but that didn't mean that he didn't consume her thoughts. Now that she was alone with her thoughts, all she thought about were the last days of her relationship with Tom. Laura found the text messages about a month before he died. Tom was sleeping and his phone continued to go off. Laura checked to see who it was before she woke Tom up. He was at the fire station for the last forty-eight hours, and she didn't want to disturb him. She decided that she had to wake him up when she saw who was calling him, though: his lover.

"Who the hell is Kathy?"

"Huh?" Tom asked groggily.

"Who the hell is Kathy?"

"She's a friend," Tom said. "I'm going back to sleep. I'm tired."

"Oh? She's a friend? Why is she calling you 'baby'?"

"What? I don't now, Laura. Jesus, will you let me sleep?"

"No. You better tell me what the hell is going on!"

"There's nothing going on, Laura. You're crazy!"

"Fine. I"ll just talk to her," Laura said. "I'll answer."

Tom jumped up from the bed and grabbed his phone from Laura's hand harshly.

"You will not touch my stuff without my permission!" Tom said. "There's no reason for this!"

"I'm not just going to let you cheat on me! I knew that we were having problems, but did it really have to come to this?" Laura asked.

"You're crazy!" Tom screamed.

Laura had never felt so horrible in her entire life. Was she not good enough for Tom? Did he not enjoy their sex together? Was the other girl prettier? Did he love the other girl? Was this the end of their family?

They spent the entire night arguing. Laura knew that he was cheating with the girl, but Tom refused to admit that he had done anything wrong. The fight went around in circles and circles. Laura started getting even more angry about Tom's refusal to talk. He tried to leave the room and the conversation every time that he got a chance. Laura would chase after him and try to get him to talk about the problem. He refused. The fight quickly turned into their repeated fight about his lack of communication. Tom left that night, and he stayed at a hotel. Soon, he came back, but they didn't talk. They lived with each other in silence. Tom would sleep in the spare room, and Laura would avoid him. The house became quiet. Dinners were quiet. They didn't bring anybody over.

Laura sat in her hotel room with take-out and tried everything she could to avoid the horrible thoughts filling her mind. She was still angry and still hurt. She hated Tom, but she missed him in the same way that she missed him before he died. Everything was so permanent now. She'd never be able to forgive him. She'd never be able to forgive herself.

*****


Laura woke up the next morning determined to move on. She was going to have to head out into town and start living her life again. She woke up, showered, got dressed, and she had some of the hotel's complimentary breakfast which consisted of orange juice, milk, coffee, muffins, and bagels. She went out into town to go explore, but she didn't really know where to go. She simply walked around to learn what was in town. There were a number of restaurants, stores, bars, and houses. It wasn't a big town, but it had a definite presence. The entire town was very country. It was new to Laura who had always lived in the suburbs. The air smelled cleaner, people smiled and waved, and people wore different clothes. They wore simple clothes, and children were playing outside instead of the kids in the suburbs who were on their computer or Xbox all day. Laura slightly cringed when she saw the firehouse in town.

Laura finally found a small diner in town and decided to get some coffee and read the help wanted ads in the paper.

"Hello!" a young woman smiled when Laura walked inside. "Will it just be you today?"

"Yes, ma'am," Laura said. "It's just me today." Laura was not used to going to a restaurant by herself. She usually had Tom with her, her mother, or one of her friends. She felt lonely.

"Well, come over here. Can I get you some coffee?" the young woman asked. She was a small girl who looked like she was barely out of high school. She wore jeans and a tee shirt with her apron.

"Yes. Please just a cup of coffee today, and I will take a local paper if you have it."

"Absolutely!" the young woman said. "Are you new in town? Or just visiting? I haven't seen you before."

"I'm new in town. Thinking of settling down here if I find the right gig," Laura said. "So here I am looking."

Laura sat down at the booth that the young woman had led her to and waited patiently for her coffee and paper. The diner was small, but it looked like a popular place for people in town to eat at on a Sunday morning. There were plenty of men and families scattered throughout the restaurant.

"Here you go," the young woman said. "Here's your coffee and your paper. My name is Jenny. I'll be back to refill your coffee in a little bit."

"Thanks, Jenny," Laura smiled. She opened the paper to the help wanted section, and she quickly realized that this was not the town for someone to get a new job. There were few opportunities, and Laura definitely wasn't qualified for most of them. She wasn't going to work in a warehouse or on a farm. She had a degree in English. That was when she saw the job opportunity for a high school teacher just one town over. Laura had gotten her teaching certificate because she figured it would be a good backup plan in case she didn't use her history degree for anything else. Laura ripped out the ad from the paper, and she finished her coffee picturing her new life as a teacher in a rural town in Kentucky. The more she looked around, the more she was liking the idea. She decided that she would spend the day sprucing up her resume, enjoy the hot tub and the pool, and turn in the resume tomorrow.

When she pulled up back into the hotel parking lot, she saw a familiar face by the entrance. She barely recognized him at first. It was the man who hugged her at the funeral. What would he be doing here? He seemed to recognize her, too. As soon as he saw her, he ran to her.

"You are not an easy woman to track down!" the man said.

Laura didn't know how to react. Why would he want to track her down so badly?

"Hi," Laura said. She was almost afraid. "I'm surprised to see you again."

"You know, you are beautiful. More beautiful than Tom ever described."

"That doesn't surprise me," Laura retorted. "He didn't really have a lot of appreciation for me when he was alive."

"I know that he did, though."

"Well, that's interesting because I never heard him tell me," Laura said.

The two were still outside of the hotel. Laura didn't appreciate where the conversation was going.

"Look, this is getting a bit heated. Let's go somewhere to talk," Gary said.

"And what do we have to talk about?" Laura asked.

"I was there the night that Tom died. I know that he'd like me to talk to you. That's why I was so determined to find you."

"Fine. There's a lake that I noticed down the road. We can go and talk there."

The lake was quiet. There was a gentle sound of water, and you could hear a cricket chirping every now and then. Laura and Gary sat down on the grass and both looked out at the lake.

"We were headed for divorce," Laura said.

"He mentioned that things weren't going that great," Gary smiled.

"Did he tell you the reason that we were going to get a divorce?" Laura asked.

"He mentioned that there was something going on. That he was talking to another girl and you found out," Gary said.

"That's a nice way to say that he's a cheating jerk. I'm only sad that he died before I was able to kill him myself," Laura snarled.

"I understand why you're angry, but it's over now. I also know he loved you."

"How could you possibly know that? Cheating on me wasn't a way to show me love. Refusing to talk to me wasn't how to show me love."

"I was with him that night."

"What night?" Laura asked.

"The night of the fire. It was one of the most horrible moments of my life. He was blockaded in the room. It only happened because the fire burned down a part of the ceiling and trapped him in the room. There was too much fire in between us. I wanted to help him, but he insisted that I had to get out before we both died. It was one of the hardest decisions of my life."

"I'm sorry that you had to go through that. You don't understand, though. Just because he was a firefighter who died in an accident, it doesn't take away from the pain from him cheating," Laura said. "It was horrible. I will never trust another person again."

"He wasn't cheating on you," Gary said. "He was talking to a friend about your problems. He couldn't open up to you. He was intimidated by you. He thought that you were brilliant, funny, and attractive. He was worried t hat if he talked to you that you would realize that he was beneath you."

"I don't believe you. If that was the case, he would have just shown me what he and Kathy were talking about," said Laura.

"He was a quiet guy. He wasn't really one to open up. You know that. Kathy is another firefighter, Laura. She's a lesbian. It was one of the only people that he could buddy up with and talk to."

"Imagine how it feels to know that your own husband can't open up to you," Laura said.

"He told me to apologize to you. He told me that he loved you. When he was stuck in the room, he told me to tell you that he loved you more than anything in this entire world. He apologized for not opening up to you. He said that he would be waiting for you," Gary said. Laura didn't say anything. "I know it was important to him for you to hear this, so I had to find you,"

Laura continued to stare out at the lake in silence. She didn't know how to respond. She thought that he was cheating this entire time. She started to feel an intense amount of guilt. Instead of enjoying their last month together, they barely spoke. Laura realized then that her last words to him were "those are mine" referring to the bottles of water in the fridge. Tears fell down her face.

*****

"Are you OK?" Gary asked, handing Laura a tissue.

"No," Laura said. "I'm not OK. I think that it was easier for me to handle his death thinking that he was a cheater. It's harder knowing that I lost a faithful and loving man."

"I know that you loved him too," Gary smiled. "He always talked about the little things you did for him. And the big ones."

"I wish that he would've expressed how much he loved me when he was alive."

"So what are you doing out here? I didn't take you for a country girl," Gary said.

"I never was a country girl. I'm really liking it out here, though. The air smells cleaner. The people are nicer. In the suburbs, the neighbors wave but talk behind your back. Here people are actually nice."

"This lake is quite pretty," Gary said. "They definitely don't have places like this in the suburbs."

"I know. Tell me about it."

"Why don't you let me hang out for a couple of days? I can help you get situated, and this way you will have someone to explore the town with," Gary said.

Laura couldn't deny that it was a tempting offer. She was lonely, and Gary could be a welcome distraction. She didn't know him, but there was something in his eyes and his face that made Laura trust him.

"Don't you need to work? They already lost one fireman," Laura asked.

"We have plenty of men on the force back home. I was thinking of helping out here for awhile. I can't imagine the fire station is too busy, but I thought I'd check and see if they need help."

"You would do that for me? I guess I could use the company."

"I'm doing it for Tom. The fact that you're beautiful and nice to talk to is only a bonus," Gary smiled. "Now, let's get out of here. I will check into the same hotel."

"I am thinking about going to apply at the high school in the next town tomorrow," Laura told him.

"Good. I"ll talk to the boys at the fire station when you do that."

Laura felt at peace for the first time in a long time. The town was so cozy, and she could live a comfortable and happy life here. It gave her a sense of relief to know that she could feel free to grieve since her husband wasn't a cheater. She lost her husband, but she didn't need to lose her happiness, too.

"This might work out well," Laura smiled. It was the first time that she realized exactly how cute Gary was. He had shaggy light brown hair and green eyes. He had large arms, and they were tattooed. He was a strong man, and Laura pictured him at the fire station lifting weights in his spare time.

Gary put his arm around Laura, and they looked out at the lake together in silence for awhile. The sound of the water made Laura relax, and she felt extremely safe in Gary's strong arms. Maybe this change of scenery was exactly what she needed. She didn't have the pitiful looks from everyone, and she wasn't constantly reminded of her old life. This place was full of new and exciting opportunities. Gary being there made it even better. He was respectful and warm. He was also the only person since Tom's death to make her feel better.

*****

When they were done talking at the lake, Laura and Gary went to the hotel to get Gary his own room. Laura was unsure of why Gary would be so generous to her, but she didn't care. She was just happy to have the help. She didn't want to admit that she was lonely and lost, but she was. Gary was also turning into quite a compatible friend. They enjoyed talking to each other, and she always respected firemen. She also thought that he could be quite funny at times.

They spent the rest of the night together. They found an Italian restaurant, and they worked out at the hotel afterward. They parted ways to their separate rooms afterward, and Laura almost invited him back into her room with her just for the company.

The next day, Laura went to the high school while Gary went to the fire station. The school was extremely receptive to Laura's resume. She had a good degree and plenty of experience. The principal said that she had not gotten anyone else nearly as qualified. The job was pretty much offered to her right there pending no problems with her references and criminal background. She walked out of the school realizing that she was starting a brand new life.

"Where are you?" Laura's mom asked.

"A small town in Kentucky. I'll send you pictures. It's absolutely beautiful."

"Well, I'm glad you went on vacation to clear your head. You have to get back into the swing of things now."

"Actually, mom. I'm thinking about staying here. I just talked to the principal of a local high school. I think I"m going to do that."

"Are you sure you want to stay in Kentucky for the rest of your life? You know there aren't any museums or theater there. I'm sure there are no nice restaurants. And you know how horrible teachers are treated, right?"

"Mom, like it here."

"But you're all alone."

"Actually, one of Gary's friends is here with me."

"Why would he come all the way out there?"

"He was here to make sure that I was OK after what happened."

"Well, that's nice." Laura could tell that her mother thought the situation was as odd as it was.

"Talk to you soon, mom. I gotta go."

Laura got back to the hotel and went immediately to Gary's room. He opened the door with a bottle of champagne in his hand.

"I don't know about you, but I will be starting at the fire station in two days!" he screamed.

"I start at the high school in a week!"

They embraced. Gary even picked Laura up a little bit. He opened the bottle of champagne, and they both jumped and cheered at the sounds of the cork popping.

"We have to celebrate. To a new life for you. To me honoring my commitments to my friend."

"Cheers!" Laura said, clinking glasses with Gary.

"Let's go out to the hot tub. It looks like fun," he said.

"Absolutely. I will go get my bathing suit on."

They were the only ones in the hot tub. It was still light out, and they stepped into the hot tub with the champagne.

"You know I'm really happy that you decided to come out. I was getting lonely," Laura told Gary.

"Fantastic. I'm glad that I'm making this easier for you. I can't imagine how it must feel to lose a spouse."

"It was one of the worst things that has ever happened to me. As angry as I was at him, he was the love of my life. It's hard to imagine that someone could be so kind and supportive. He always wanted me to be happy in whatever I did, and he was a great provider."

"I know he was a great guy. That's why I was so insistent on coming out here to see you. It's hard to lose a brother. It's even worse to practically watch it happen."

"Let's talk about anything else," Laura said after a moment of silence.

"How about us?"

"Us?"

"Yes. Us," Gary prodded.

"I don't know what you're talking about," Laura said nervously.

"I know that you feel it too," Gary said. "We have a natural attraction to each other."

Laura couldn't deny it. Gary was attractive and kind. She was starting to feel attracted to him. She started feeling it when they were sitting by the lake. He was so understanding, and she could actually talk to him. It was hard for her to admit her real feelings. However, Laura wanted to make sure that she wasn't just attracted to Gary because she was lonely and vulnerable after the death.

"I think that we should take it slowly," Laura said quietly. "I'm so far away from home. I also think that I'm going to stay here and take the job as a teacher."

"I will stay here too."

"Don't you have any reasons to stay back home? Family? Friends?"

"I have a bigger reason to stay here," Gary looked at Laura longingly. "You're so strong, and you're so beautiful. I want to be here for you. Who else would you have?"

"I appreciate your kindness, but I can do this on my own," Laura said. "I lost a husband, but I'm still relatively young. I also knew that this was part of the deal by marrying a fireman."

"That doesn't mean that you have to do it alone," Gary said.

"And what if you get hurt in a fire too? I don't think that I can go through that again."

"Look, it was my fault for bringing it up. I came here to tell you how much Tom loved you, and I've done that. Here, I'm starting to look like a prune. Let's get out of here."

"Yeah. I can actually stand to relax for the rest of the night. It was nice to have someone to celebrate with, though," Laura told Gary.

"We have plenty to celebrate. I'll still be here for a couple of weeks. I want to make sure that you adjust OK. You know what room I'm in."

With that, Laura got out of the hot tub and went to relax in her hotel room for the rest of the night.

*****

Laura and Gary stopped talking as much. They would get coffee in the hotel lounge in the morning and talk casually. They would also take Daisy out for walks together sometimes. Gary started at the fire station, and he loved it. The men were easy to get along with, and the fire station really needed him. His days were filled with rogue cigarettes igniting curtains. Laura was happy that Gary was able to help at the fire station while he was here. It was also nice to have a friend. The only other friend Laura had was Jenny at the diner.

The diner was one of the places that Laura started to feel comfortable in town. She walked in and Jenny immediately smiled and brought her a cup of coffee. Laura always went there when Gary was at the fire station in the morning. One particular morning Laura walked into the diner. Jenny was there as always.

"Hi!" Jenny waved. "I"ll go ahead and get you your coffee."

"Thank you!" Laura said cheerily, making her way to a small booth she liked to sit at.

"Are you gonna have breakfast this morning?" Jenny asked, putting down the coffee.

"Sure. I'm going to have a 2x2x2. Scrambled eggs and sausage," Laura said.

"Getting sick of the muffins and bagels at the hotel?" Jenny asked.

"Yes! It's fine, but eating here is so much better," Laura told her.

Suddenly, one of the guests at the diner got up in a hurry and ran to Jenny.

"I gotta go," he said. "There's a huge fire down the road, and they need all the help they can get. I need you to give me my tab now."

"Just go," Jenny said. "I will take care of this one for you."

"Thank you," the man said, and he ran out the diner and into his truck.

"My friend is at the fire station right now. I hope the fire isn't too bad," Laura said worriedly.

"Let me put on the news," Jenny said.

Laura followed Jenny to be as close to the television as possible and saw the huge fire on the news. A small house was completely engulfed in flames. The fire was the top story on every local news channel. Laura sat in fear watching the scene. Her mind filled with memories of Tom's death. She was filled with fear for Gary. She silently prayed for his safety and continued to watch for any new news.

The news went on to say that there was still one person left in the house. It made Laura sick, and she didn't want to watch anymore, but she had to make sure that Gary was alright. The story went on to say that there was still a person that they were trying to remove from the burning building. The following update advised the watchers that the person stuck in the building was a fireman.

Laura ran out of the diner without saying anything, and she drove to the site of the fire. She ran from the car, but she had to wait behind the caution tape and watch the action from a safe distance. She tried not to cry while looking for Gary. She didn't see him.

Finally, she saw Gary walking from the now smokey building with a small dog in his hands. He stayed in the building to bring the puppy to safety. Seeing him emerge from the building was the happiest that Laura had ever been. It was like she was watching Tom come back to life.

Laura ran past the caution tape despite the consequences and hugged Gary. He was in his fire suit, and he smelled like intense smoke. She didn't care what he smelled like. She was just happy that he was alive. She took off his helmet and kissed him. Happy tears fell down her cheek, and she hugged him again.

"I thought that I was going to lose you, too," Laura said into his large chest.

"I wasn't going to let that happen," Gary said. "I promised Tom that I was going to take care of you."

"You don't have to do that," Laura said.

"I know. I want to."

"What are you saying?"

"I'm saying that I have already told the fire station that I am planning on taking a permanent position. We can start a life out here together."

"Isn't it a bit too soon?"

"We'll go slow if you want. We can get separate places at first," Gary said. "Whatever you think is the best. I'm willing to go at your pace."

"Let's go. We can spend the rest of the day talking about our future together," Laura said.

"I can't," Gary laughed. "I have to complete the rest of my shift. I'll come see you as soon as I'm done with work. Now go on before you get us both in trouble. You're not supposed to cross the tape."

Laura kissed him one more time and went back to the diner.

"Where did you go?" Jenny asked.

"I had to go to the fire and make sure my friend Gary was OK."

"I knew that you were too invested in the fire," Jenny said. "I was going to find you at the hotel to give you your bill."

"I wasn't going to do that to you, Jenny. And you better get used to me. I think I'm going to be here for a long time."

Laura was one of the most popular teachers in the entire high school, and Gary became a quick captain at the fire house. The wedding was around the same time at a beautiful farm in the area.They moved into into a small three bedroom house and their first son was born about a year later.

www.ingramcontent.com/pod-product-compliance
Lightning Source LLC
Chambersburg PA
CBHW020324180726
47991CB00018B/659